THE LAST DROP

CULLEN & BAIN 6

ED JAMES

PROLOGUE

Dale

That girl was bad news. Turning up on a first date with a bottle of sambuca. Dale's head thumped and he still tasted the aniseed burn.

Why was it so dark?

Or, when did it get so dark?

Go out for a few drinks in the park, then it turns into the black of night.

Dale checked his watch. Half eight. What? He tried walking on, but Christ, his legs weren't listening.

She looked hot on poggr, but in real life she was *smoking*. And small, just how he liked them. Dale's long shadow stretching out on the pavement ahead of him, thick and bulky like he thought he was.

He fished his phone out of his pocket and, yes! Her number was there. Saved by the date, 2021-05-04. He'd obviously been too far gone to note down her name on the contact, and all he had was her name on that poggr app.

Foxyminx2259

What was her real name again?

Anna? Eva? Evelyn?

Ah well. He had ways and means of getting that out of her. Little tricks he'd picked up over the years.

And she knew how to play him. 'Let's meet up again soon.'

Sure thing, darling.

Dale turned onto the Grassmarket, not far from home. The shop offered a special on cans of WakeyWakey. Way too late for it now, but maybe he should stock up for the inevitable hangover.

But, no, he should just get back home.

Still, all he could think of was Foxyminx2259, that wee blonde girl from Granton who liked speaking to a postgraduate Philosophy student rather than making a joke about it.

Dale stopped at the crossing and checked his bag was still wrapped around him. Super tight—nobody was getting what was in it. Killing two birds with one stone, meeting her in Princes Street Gardens just after he'd met his *man* for the latest delivery. He patted the bag, but had to lean against the metal pole, still roasting from the hot day.

The Last Drop bar was shut. Usually, he'd head in there, sup on a pint of Guinness, milk some fake Irish blarney charm for all he was worth. Lockdown was over, maybe, but half eight was last orders. Barbaric!

And that sambuca…

Christ.

A man staggered towards him, wearing a maroon Hearts top and a scowl, the kind that was like he knew Dale and didn't exactly have a high opinion of him. Still, he walked on past, shaking his bald head.

Aye. Dale needed his bed. A cup of tea, a bath, then his bed. Ideally in that order.

While The Last Drop was shut, some lights were on just around the corner, a few steps from his flat. The Debonair was always open, even at the tail end of a pandemic.

Maybe he should get that cup of tea now, maybe with a wee tot of whisky in it.

He shuffled up close enough and kept hold of his bag.

A load of tables outside, the chairs all tipped up and resting on top. In the daytime, as long as you didn't mind second-hand cigarette smoke and the hissing of bus brakes, it was all good. Back to something like normal. Banter, chat, drinking, but debauchery would have to wait, in public at least.

Now, though, it was shut. Not even a bouncer to keep people like Dale away.

One of the tables had been missed by the clear-up, though. Someone had been kind enough to leave behind a copy of the *Edinburgh Argus* and the best part of a bottle of red and a glass.

Waste not, want not.

A bit of lipstick never killed anyone, least of all Dale.

Dale splashed some wine into the glass and still had a good bit left in the bottle. Smelled nice, all meaty and solid, and tasted pretty sharp.

Glorious!

Dale kicked back and flicked open the Argus, getting just enough overhead light to read it. This is the life. He checked the front page. Well, *he* didn't need to drive to Barnard Castle to test how bad his eyesight was. Everything was a blur. He tossed the paper down and sat back, sipping the wine.

This *is* the life.

Something thumped behind him.

Dale craned his neck around, rocking the chair to the side and almost toppling over onto the slabs.

Another thump.

Two women were staring out at him from inside the bar, distorted by the glass. Clutching wine glasses, dolled up like they were out clubbing. Same uniform, like they were in Munich for Oktoberfest. One thinner than the other, but both pretty enough, even with face masks hanging from their chins. Either would do.

Dale flashed a smile at the smaller one. Dark hair, and he got a very dark smile in return.

Oh, she was trouble.

He toasted her with his glass.

She opened the door and peered out. 'We're shut.'

He waved a finger at her, squinting hard. 'Do I know you from somewhere?'

And his heart skipped a beat—maybe he did recognise her. Maybe she was 17th August 2019, or 23rd March 2020, or 25th April 2020. Slightly naughty meeting during a lockdown, but they said it was just a 'flu, especially in the young.

Right?

Nah, Dale would've remembered her. Those hazelnut eyes, that cute smile, it screamed of the things she wanted done to her.

She stepped out onto the slabs, tilting her head to the side. 'Don't *think* so.' She was sipping a glass of white wine, chilling the edge. 'Do you recognise him, Becks?'

Her mate joined her. No social distancing with these two. A touch more makeup than Dale liked. Becks—Becky? Rebecca? Rebekah?—gave a shrug. 'Nuh.' Not so much a no as a grunt.

'But I recognise you.' The first one slurped vino collapso. 'You ever come in here?'

'Usually go to the Last Drop, but it's not open.'

'Nor are we.' Becky smiled, like she was flirting. 'But that's not an answer.'

'Been in a few times, aye.' Dale checked his bag was still at his feet. 'Quite a nice wee place.'

'You ever go to Club Astra?'

'A few times. Maybe that's where I recognise you from.'

She's acting all coy now. 'Maybe.' Looking away, all pretend indifference.

Becky sipped more wine. 'Maybe I spoke to you before all that shite happened.'

'Doubt that.' Dale splashed out some more red. God, it was going down as fast as his thumping headache was slipping away. He gave her *that* smile. No doubt about it, the little minx would—

Dale decided to say it out loud. 'I'm guessing you've spent a few Saturday nights in there bopping to chart music. Right?'

'Right.' She nodded. 'Totally. But before lockdown, eh?'

'Right, right.' Aye, Dale knew her sort. Very vanilla. But the other one, the shorter one, she had a bit of an edge to her. And Becky was way too keen. Dale enjoyed the sport, relished chasing prey that's resistant to the hunt. So he focused on her, giving her his all. 'But you're not too keen, are you?'

'Right. I mean, I love dancing but the music's not my bag. Get enough of that shite in here.' She waved behind her into the bar, then took another sip of wine.

'So what's your speed, darling? Indie? Hip hop? Dubstep?'

She scowled at him. 'What's dubstep?'

'Absolutely awful.' Dale laughed, but it sounded like a giggle, a bit too high-pitched to be macho. But it was enthusiastic and she seemed to like enthusiastic. 'So, what, The Killers? Celine Dion?'

'The Killers more than Celine Dion.'

Becky huffed. 'I'm going back in. Place doesn't clean itself. Coming, Nina?'

Nina. That was an absolutely nailed-on name for her. Nina. The minx. 'Be a sec, Becks.' She smiled as her pal slipped inside.

'Nina, eh?' Dale took his glass over to stand next to her. Almost fell over and took the glass with him, but he managed to stay upright. He stood where he could keep an eye on his bag. 'Gorgeous name.'

'You think?'

'Sure. And it suits you.' He held out his hand. 'Dale.'

Despite all that hands-face-space advice from the government, she took it without so much as a squirt of sanitiser. 'Nina. Pleased to meet you.'

Dale could've pointed out that he already knew, but it was a good gauge of how wankered she was. 'Wee glass of white wine after work, yeah?'

'We're allowed to. Helps with all the cleaning, like. Absolutely starving, mind.'

'I could eat too.' Dale held her gaze a few seconds. 'What do you like to eat?'

Nina looked over the rim of her glass. 'Sausage.'

Dale nodded. 'Oh aye? Big fat sausages?'

'Just one at a time.' She giggled. 'Except that time in Crete.'

Dale leaned forward, but almost stumbled. 'Tell me more.'

The door thudded open again and Becky stormed out. 'He's here.'

A frown danced across Nina's forehead. 'Seriously?' She looked around the place like she was going to have to run.

Becky swallowed then nodded. 'Seriously.'

Nina peered inside the pub. 'Looks fine to me.'

'*He's* here, Nina. He's here!'

Dale turned to burp into his hand, then rested his hand on Nina's arm, casually but with enough contact to let her know he was there to protect her. 'Who's here?'

'The ghost.' Nina was rolling her eyes. 'Becky thinks this place is haunted by the previous owner.'

Becky had the look of the zealot, someone who was sure of their mad belief and wanted everyone to share in it. 'Nobody knows how he died!'

'That's bullshit, Becks.' Nina laughed, a bit too hard, like all the tension had gone. 'He was dealing coke. No, *supplying* coke.'

Dale took a wee look at the bag. Still there.

'Pissed off the wrong guy, he killed him. The cops caught the killer.' Nina frowned. 'Might've even been a cop.'

Dale sipped wine but spilt more than he drank, sluicing down his cheeks. He managed to wipe it away without anyone noticing. 'Could go some coke just now.'

Becky rolled her eyes at him. 'Bar's shut. And we only have Pepsi.'

'Why don't you get me a can, then? One of those wee ones you get on the plane?'

Becky looked back at the door, then swallowed. 'Okay.' She went back in, but she was clearly terrified of the ghost of the Debonair.

Nina wrapped her hand around Dale's arm. 'You, eh, got some *coke* coke?'

'The real thing.'

'I mean, not the stuff that comes in red cans.'

Dale patted his pocket. But he had to sit down. The sambuca and the wine were playing merry hell with everything. He wrapped his feet around the bag. Protect that with his life. 'Might have access to a wee bit, aye.'

Nina looked at him, then inside the bar. She licked her lips and finished the glass of wine. 'You fancy talking more back at mine?'

Dale tapped the table. 'Sold!' He sank the rest of his glass. 'Whereabouts?'

Nina pursed her lips, raised her eyebrows and nodded over the road. 'Above Farooq's.'

Dale clicked his fingers. 'That'll be where I know you from. I'm in there all the time. His raw turmeric is *excellent*.'

'You a chef or something?'

'No, but I think I'm cooking on gas here.' Dale held out a hand. 'Lead on, my lady.'

'Nina!' Becky was back outside the bar, holding a bottle of Pepsi Max. 'Where are you going?'

'For a lie down.'

'But I've just opened another bottle of—'

'Sure you'll drink it all yourself.' Nina grabbed Dale's hand and squeezed it. 'She's just jealous.' She led him away from the bar.

'Hey, you've forgotten your bag!'

Shite!

DALE FELT like he was being kissed by an octopus. Her hands were *everywhere*. All over his back, on his ding dong, grabbing his face. He had to break off from her to breathe. He leaned over the coffee table and took another toot of coke through the twenty-pound note. A bit sharp against his skin, but God damn, that was good stuff. 'You stay here on your own?'

Nina's flat looked like an art gallery. Wooden floors and white walls, filled with a triptych of red and green and blue artworks. Signed and looked to be originals.

She finished her own line, hungrier than he was. 'No, I rent the spare room to Becky.'

'You own it?'

'Something like that.' Her eyes were looking for another go as she rubbed at her nose.

Dale tipped some coke out of his baggie and started chopping up more lines. Longer ones, but not what they'd call Hollywood lines. This grade of coke, you'd burst your septum in *minutes*. 'After you.'

She hoovered it up in one long go. 'Oh this is good shit. Where did you get it?'

'A gentleman doesn't talk.'

'Are you saying you're a gentleman?'

'Hardly.' Dale leaned over and snorted half the line, then offered it to her.

She bent over and took it all. She was unreal!

'So you come from money, then, Nina?'

'C'mere.' She bit his bottom lip and tugged off his T-shirt.

'Wow, you're ripped.'

'Despite all my drinking, aye. And I'm a bit off my best.'

'Seriously?'

'Seriously.'

Now she was at his belt, working away at the thing. Felt like she was squashing him. 'I want to suck your cock.'

'I want you to as well, baby.'

Dale eased off the belt catch and let his jeans go.

Nina was on the floor now, tugging at his boxers.

But absolutely nothing was happening down there.

That glass of wine on top of all that sambuca and last night's beer and today's water... Even that quality of coke couldn't cut through all that.

Actually, maybe he needed a piss.

Dale pushed away but she was pinning him down. 'I need to go to the little boy's room.'

'I thought we were going to—'

'Just need the bathroom.' Dale managed to pry himself away from her squid-like grip and looked around. 'Which way?'

Nina was sitting back on the sofa now, just in her bra and panties. When did that happen? She flicked a hand to the side.

Dale couldn't see a door. He walked closer and had to brace himself against the wall. Aha, there it was, inset into the bookcase. 'Just a pee, then we'll be good to go. Okay?'

She was gorgeous, but he was in no state to give her all of his loving. 'Just hurry up.'

His bag was on the floor. Good. Dale pushed through and shut the door behind him.

Christ.

He even had to sit down to pee. A trickle at first, then a gush. And it just didn't stop. He held onto the toilet paper roll holder to keep upright.

The sink was covered in toiletries. Posh ones. That brand he saw in hotels when his parents took him away.

He was finished. Finally. So he stood up and washed his hands. Then he looked at his wanger and it was having none of it. The coke should've made it rise like a flagpole, but nope. It wasn't even at half-mast.

He shook it a bit.

Nothing.

Christ, he was twenty-four. He shouldn't be having erectile disfunction.

Brewer's droop, wasn't it?

And distiller's... droop?

Vintner's Viagra! That's what he needed.

Shagging that girl last night hadn't been a problem. Had to be the booze. Too much, and not enough sleep.

He needed to sober up. And fast. Then he'd be hard enough to give Nina everything she wanted.

An ice-cold bath would do the trick!

He turned the bath tap to right under the blue sign then kept going, and turned it up full blast. Freezing cold water started flowing out. He stripped down to his birthday suit and sipped cold water from the sink tap.

Christ, the bath was full already! Either the taps were on full flow or he'd blacked out. Either was possible.

He turned it off and put his left foot in. He almost shrieked.

Man up!

He put his right in and felt his balls tighten.

Christ, it was working!

He was breathing hard and fast, though.

He sat down, quick and dirty, like that big German guy from the gym told him. Get in there, don't think about it.

He felt his heart thudding, deep and regular, but it was slow and slowing down.

He lay back in the big tub and almost shrieked again as the cold sliced up his back.

Then he put his head under.

Ten seconds.

And he was up again, gasping for breath. Freezing cold now. He felt like a corpse.

Something was stirring down there. Little Dale was back!

He heard something from the flat, maybe the front door.

Probably nothing. Maybe Nina was fed up of him already. Or maybe she'd gone to get some more booze from Farooq. Probably enough time to get a bottle of Rioja to go with the Bolivian Marching Powder.

Dale lay back in the bath and stuck his head back under the water, eyes shut. Twenty seconds this time.

He pushed up, gasping in air, and reopened his eyes.

The room was pitch black.

Something battered off his temple.

1

SHEPHERD

It had been a few years since Luke Shepherd had walked into a pub and had a crowd of mates waiting for him. Pals, friends, colleagues, whatever. But here he was, stepping inside the Cheeky Judge pub to meet up with some people.

The air smelled of soured beer and stale sweat. A fire crackled and spit, a haze of smoke hanging in the air. Heat radiated off the walls, making the place sweat. The windows were covered over to stop prying eyes seeing inside. Without the fire, the place would seem as cold and dark as a cave.

Four drinkers. One at the bar, one in the window and two huddled around a table at the back, their voices barking with a guttural sound.

Shepherd didn't want to be here, but *they* were so he couldn't be anywhere else. He'd given so much to the cause over the years, to rooting out bent cops. And he needed to know what the daft sods were saying to each other. After all, the walls had ears in this place.

He walked up to the horseshoe bar and caught the attention of the barman, loading up the dishwasher, but with enough builder's cleavage to park a police motorbike. He looked around at Shepherd, nodded, then took a few attempts to stand up. 'Oof, son, getting old's a bastard.' He wore a black mask with The Crafty Butcher emblazoned on it.

Shepherd clocked him through the fabric. Willie McAllister. An old Leith uniform plod. Useless sod, except for getting him to block doorways or fetch cups of tea. 'Take your word for it.' He leaned across the taps. 'Your boss in?'

'Might be.'

Shepherd nodded, then stepped back. 'Get us an orange juice.'

'You know we're shut and you should have your mask on.'

'Double jabbed and the door's wide open. Fire's on too.'

'Brazen, son, brazen.' McAllister reached for a glass and his belly flopped out of his T-shirt. 'Bring it over to you.'

'Cheers.' Shepherd opened his jacket and got a waft of his own sweat. Christ, that fire was completely unnecessary on a day like this. Only useful for burning evidence. He walked over to the table and sat.

DI Scott Cullen sat at the opposite end. Shepherd's boss, but seven years younger. And he looked it. Trim, clean-shaven and with a haircut that'd lost none of its sharpness during the lockdown. 'Evening, Luke.'

'Scott.' Shepherd noticed Willie approaching with his orange juice and took it before the bead of sweat on Willie's forehead dropped into the glass. 'Cheers.'

DC Craig Hunter waved a hand in front of Willie's face, but missed. A big lump, his skinhead adding another level of menace. 'Another two pints of the IPA, chief.'

Willie scowled into the mirror filling the wall behind them, advertising a long-dead Edinburgh brewery, then smiled. 'Coming right up, lads.' He waddled off to the bar.

'Evening, Sarge.' Hunter sank the last of his beer and kept his focus on the empty glass. 'Busy day?'

'Nope.' Shepherd cradled the glass, sucking all the cold out of it. Or was it the other way round, that it sucked the heat out of him? He didn't know, but the sweat was pooling in parts he'd rather not think about. 'One of those days where bugger all happens.'

'Even in a pandemic, eh?' Hunter looked right at Cullen. 'Need to get off sharp tonight. Running a raid on the Debonair in the morning.'

Shepherd dropped his glass without spilling much and grabbed Hunter's big arm, leaning in close to whisper, 'Craig, you shouldn't be talking about that to officers not on the operation.'

'Aye, aye, aye.' Hunter brushed him off. He was swaying a bit and slurring a lot. He snarled, baring long teeth. 'Saw Kenny Falconer in prison last week. Guy walks with a limp because of what I did to him. I almost...' He shut his eyes.

'Craig...' Cullen looked at Shepherd. 'Why don't you—' His phone blared out. He picked it up and stared at the display, holding it for a few seconds, before shuffling to his feet. 'Shite. It's the boss. Back in a minute.' He walked off through the empty bar.

Shepherd could've grabbed Hunter's arm again, like he'd done back in the day. But this was his grave, not anybody else's. Well, maybe Cullen's.

Shepherd drank the bitter orange juice, grateful for the ice in this stifling heat. 'You doing okay down there, Craig?'

'Define okay...' Hunter shoved his hands in his pockets. 'You must be happy you've shunted me and Malky McKeown off to the drugs squad. Got rid of two clowns from your team, eh?' He picked up his glass, tried to drink from it, then noticed it was empty and slammed it back down. He shot Willie a scowl. 'I'm finding it difficult, if you must know.'

'Thought you'd like working that beat, Craig.'

'It's not a beat. It's sitting in an office, listening to recordings that you can't hear properly. Over and over again.'

Hunter wasn't happy unless he was beating people up or chasing them.

'Still, it'll be good experience.'

'One thing I've got more than enough of.' Hunter looked over at the bar. 'Willie, those pints coming?'

'Aye, aye, hold your horses, champ.'

Hunter narrowed his eyes and tilted his head in the direction of the side window, the only one that wasn't blocked up. 'Could've sworn that was Charlie Kidd and Malky McKeown. What's that about?'

Shepherd had a look himself but it was dark out there. 'I don't know, Craig. Maybe you're seeing things. That's what happens when you down pints on an empty stomach.'

Hunter laughed. 'Thing is, Sarge, they've got us working on this new drug lord running Edinburgh. After what happened to the old one, anyone picking up that baton will be a very brave man.'

'Or woman.'

Hunter nodded. 'True, but it's a man.' He snorted with laughter. Christ, he was blootered. 'Me and Malky got sent around this place in Muirhouse. Usual deal, reinforced steel doors, bricked-up windows. Spells D-E-A-L-E-R, right?' He waited for Shepherd to nod. 'Trouble for Dave the Animal was that his customers waiting outside were respecting social distancing. Two metres apart.'

Shepherd couldn't help but laugh. 'That's priceless.'

'Tell me about it. Arrested a good chunk of them too. Dave the Animal has been in hiding since lockdown. Heard whispers of where he was, but couldn't find him. So it was good to catch him red-handed. Bursting in there with four uniformed sods, their bodycams recording him taking a hundred quid in exchange for a load of cocaine. Got him speaking about stuff, but not naming any names. Just detailing the operation, providing intel. It's a bloke, but that's it. So frustrating. But we've got a warrant for first thing tomorrow.'

'Well, good luck. And maybe don't shoot your mouth off in here, aye?'

But Hunter was looking behind him.

Cullen wandered back, cradling two pints and carrying a packet of nuts between his teeth. He spat the bag onto the table. 'Sorry, boys, but Davenport's caught a murder case. Body in a bath just off the Grassmarket.'

Hunter folded his arms. 'Scott, I'm too pissed for duty.'

'Aye, Craig, and you're not on my team just now. But me and Shepherd are on.' Cullen rested the pints in front of him. 'You don't *have* to drink both of these, okay?'

'I'll see how I do.' Hunter picked them both up and wandered back to the bar and Willie McAllister.

Cullen was looking at him with the expression of a disappointed uncle or older brother. But he didn't say anything, instead turning to Shepherd. 'Let's get out of here before I hear him saying something I'll regret.'

2

BAIN

Beauty of these massive mirrors is, if you know a boy or two, you can turn them into two-way jobs, just like in the police station. Back when I was a cop.

Christ sake.

Anyway.

The three big bastards are all there.

Hunter over by the bar, his huge frame like he could do some damage to you in a phone box if he attacked you from behind.

Aye, I know all about that.

Cullen with that short-sleeved shirt, showing off his disco muscles. Boy's been hitting the press-ups hard over lockdown, I tell you. He tugs his leather biker jacket and it's a wee bit too tight, isn't it? Tart. 'I'll see you down there, Luke.'

The sound is immaculate, like. I think it's even clearer than if you were standing between them.

'Aye, just need to go to the toilet.' Shepherd claps Hunter on the arm. 'Mind what I said.'

He might, but I don't. Shepherd was smart enough to whisper. Knew he was being listened to, didn't he?

But Craig Hunter... Nah, he's scubbed.

Loose lips sink ships and all that.

Willie will loosen them further. Got that triple IPA to offer him. Nine and a half percent, tastes like gun oil with a bit of pineapple and grapefruit. Gorgeous, but don't drink too much of it. No, Craig will.

I sit back and take in the office. My office. My lair. Makes me cackle, but I can't stop it.

Bare walls, no pictures or posters, no knick-knacks or family heirlooms. Just the bare minimum—a desk, a computer and some world-class recording equipment. Dust motes hang in the air, dancing in the dirty light. Place reeks of pish too. Joy of one of the walls facing the urinals and Willie not bothering to pay that cleaning bill, seven times.

Can't get the staff.

Still, he's got other uses.

And it's the perfect base of operations to take revenge on those pricks.

I take a sip of that non-alcoholic IPA I picked up. Swear, you can't tell the difference. Smells like an explosion in a fruit shop, but tastes dark and bitter.

Gorgeous!

Christ, I miss doing that podcast.

Why did Elvis have to be such a fanny about everything?

Why does everyone have to be such a fanny about everything?

But the alcohol was dulling my senses, making me miss what was in front of us. So I'm a clean man now.

The door opens and Shepherd slides into my office, stepping across the stained lino. Doesn't sit, just leans against the back of the chair opposite us. 'Well?'

Another sip. God, need to get this on tap. 'Well, well.'

'Brian...' Shepherd huffs into the chair, folding his giant arms. Definitely doesn't need to be wearing that massive coat in here, not with the fire on hot enough to burn the air. 'You lured them here, didn't you?'

'Lure's a bit strong...'

'Still, an after-hours lock-in taking place in a police bar?'

'Already got some cracking material, like.'

He drums his fingers on the table. 'Anything I can use?'

I wave over at the computer. 'Sadly not. Some big copper told me not to record what people say.' I point at the screen where the daft sod is letting himself go. 'Still, would've been nice to have heard what you said to him.'

Shepherd looks at us, then the bottle, then back at us, licking his lips. 'Brian, if all you can offer me is old news and more lies from the past then we're—'

'Oh, come on, Lukey-baby. That's not all and you know it.'

'No, you've got drunken police officers in a bar all talking. Tell me you're not recording it.'

'Tried, but it was all gibberish. Worse than an army of goblins at the bottom of a well. You couldn't pick out anything.'

He laughs. 'What about Craig Hunter tonight?'

That look again, like it's drilling into my skull, enough to make me want to drink again. 'You should do him for chucking Kenny Falconer off the roof.'

'Like I say, Brian. Old news.'

'Old news, my arse!' I slam the bottle down and beer fizzes out of the top. 'I was there! Hunter almost killed Falconer! Cullen had to stop him. Ended up hurting himself, the stupid prick.'

The boy narrows his eyes. He's like a wee trout in the river thinking he'd love to bite on the worm, but he's not sure it's juicy enough.

I sip down the foam. 'Cullen stood up for Hunter, right after he'd porked his bird.'

He sits there, arms folded again, thinking and thinking hard. 'And you were the one who backed them up, Brian. DI

Bain, lord of his realm and the idiot running the show. You backed him up. Both of them. Could've drummed them both off the force if you'd told the truth.'

I tear at the bottle's label, revealing a bit more brown and the paper's stuck to the side. 'Aye, and how well did that turn out?' I finish the bottle and reach over for another one. 'So, you're not going to do them?'

'Brian, I can't. You've got nothing on them.'

The last words in the world I want to ear. Or expect to. I tear the lid off the next bottle and only graze my skin a little bit. 'You know what those two pricks did to me, Luke? I was a DI. I ran a team. Solved crimes. I should be the DCI, not Ally bloody Davenport! Then I got demoted, kicked through the Glasgow. Then, when I was down, they did it again. A DC! Me! And that big arsehole smashed me in a phone box.'

'Brian, that was investigated. Fully. Hunter *was* on camera, but he was walking away from the scene long before your attack happened. He denied everything and there were no witnesses. Hard as it is for an ex-cop, you need to accept that it was a random act of violence. Sure you've got enough enemies out there?'

'Don't tell me I brought it all on myself, Luke. Because I didn't. Christ's sake. It's entirely on them and that useless prick Methven.'

Shepherd stares hard at us, like he's figured something out. 'Colin Methven will never walk again.'

I shrug. 'So? He's a prick. Deserves it.'

Shepherd laughs. 'You're something else.'

'Luke, my *intel* has told you where the bodies are buried. So find them!'

'I can't do that, Brian. Sorry.'

'Hang on. I gave you all this evidence, a DCI in the Complaints, and all you can do is shoot me in the foot?'

Shepherd holds his thumb up. 'One, I'm not a DCI in

Professional Standards and Ethics, I'm a DS in the Major Investigation Team.' Forefinger plus a really smarmy raised eyebrow. Prick. 'Two, you've shot *yourself* in the foot, not me.' He frowns now, like he's run out of points to make.

I take a long drink of the fake beer. 'So you've got no more—'

'And three,' middle finger pointing at us, 'you'll be criminally liable for broadcasting illicitly obtained recordings on that podcast.'

I raise my shoulders. 'Only podcast I did was about beer. Sorry, Luke. Not me.'

He narrows his eyes at me, but doesn't say anything.

'Don't look at me like that!' I slam the beer down again and this one scooshes everywhere. Christ! 'I should be *raging* at you! You've been at this for almost a whole year and still got no juice on Cullen and Hunter!'

Looks like he's about to spill something, but gets to his feet now, staring at us, his raised eyebrows like a stack of bacon on his forehead. 'Brian, I suggest you desist from this.'

Red rag to a bull!

We're onto something here.

'Sure thing, Luke. Aye.'

'I mean it. If you publish any material recorded here, the only thing you'll accomplish is getting arrested. No consent from any of the parties involved means any recordings in here are illegal.'

'I'm not that stupid. Like I said, the recordings were inaudible. But I do have sources who come into the bar, credible sources, cops even, eager to talk about our friends. And on the record. But I can't divulge those recordings yet.'

Shepherd walks over to the door and jabs a finger at me. 'I'm serious. Let it go. There's nothing there. You'll just get yourself into trouble.'

'Noted.' I give him a nod and watch the door closing behind

him. Then wait a few seconds until I see the big bastard striding through the pub.

I sit there, thinking it all through. I've been feeding him shite, under the radar, and he hasn't made the link to that podcast. Well, if he's backing away from the active investigation, I'm going to have to step up to the plate, eh?

But I can't listen to the recordings, either. Absolute pish. I really need to get Elvis in here to set up the system better, but I can't risk tipping him off if he goes offside. Like he's prone to. Wee grassing bastard. And the other clown I'm working with isn't exactly blessed as an engineer.

Someone knocks on the door.

'Come in.'

But nobody does.

'Bugger me.' I get up and go see who it is.

Malky McKeown's standing there, scratching his balls like he's still got crabs. His eyebrows still haven't grown back from that stag weekend. Daft twat.

'Come on in. You're amongst friends now.'

He looks at us and frowns, whispering, 'Luke's in here.'

'He left'

'Oh, right.' He thumbs behind him.

Charlie Kidd, that big streak of pish with a ponytail down to his arse. IT Forensics Officer. He gives us a nod, 'Brian,' then takes a seat.

Malky stays by the door, hand in his trousers. Scratching away. 'Charlie's got something.'

'Hopefully not pubic lice.' I sit forward, leaning across the desk. Used to work a treat back when I was a cop. 'What've you got to say for yourself?'

'Just...' Kidd swings his ponytail like he's trying to attach a rope to a mooring slot. 'Some shite that went down way back when.'

'When are we talking?'

'Ten years ago.'

Kidd nods. 'Think I've got a way for you to screw over Scott and Craig.'

I lean forward. 'Go on.'

'Something on Yvonne Flockhart.'

'She would've been Hunter's girlfriend at the time.' I nod, like one of those wee dogs in the back of a car. 'But she's Cullen's lady now.' Almost rub my hands together, but that'd be jinxing it. I look over at Kidd. 'Go on.'

Kidd rests his ponytail on his shoulder like it's his pet snake. 'Got her audit trail records for the Monday morning after that incident.' He folds his arms, shaking his head. 'Yvonne searched for a "Jennifer Carnegie".'

'Christ's sake.' I slump back in the chair. '*You've* searched now?'

Kidd looks like he's just started high school and all his mates have found new pals. 'I could get into deep shite for even looking!'

'She could be anyone, you clown! Just tell them that.'

Kidd looks around at us. 'You think that's going to wash? Because it won't. I need more money, Brian.'

'And here we are. There's gold in that thar Jennifer Carnegie.'

Malky sidles up now, still adjusting his jeans. 'This is my fault, Bri. Got him to repeat that search I did. Charlie's got access to other channels. The interesting thing is she's a Person of Interest in a child abuse case running back in the nineties. Up in Angus.'

Kidd's frowning. 'That's good, is it?'

I nod. 'Cullen grew up in Angus.'

'Sure?' Kidd sits back. 'I'm a Dundee boy and I thought he was Edinburgh.'

'No, he's Dalhousie.'

'Right.' He stares blankly, like that makes sense now.

Malky's still itching. 'Well, the upshot of it is we've got her new name and a current address.'

I shoot to my feet and punch the air like the Gers have just scored against those green-and-white tatty-picking bastards. 'YAAASSS!'

3

CULLEN

Cullen would've thought that wearing a mask every time he was out in public would make suiting up for a crime scene a bit easier, but no. At least it tasted of fruity gum rather than the stale beer. Just one pint meant he could drive, meant he could work. But he was a sweaty mess by the time he'd signed the clipboard. He needed to change his shirt.

The living room was like a gallery. Bare, functional. The sofa was wooden pallets resting on stone blocks with some cushions on top. The coffee table matched. Could be homemade, could be expensive designer stuff. Either way, getting it up the stairs would've been a killer. Still, at least it was above a shop rather than someone's house.

And that was it.

Just some paintings on the stark white walls. Music played, some filthy nineties Prince, but there were no obvious speakers in the room.

The window looked down to the Grassmarket, that home of stag and hen parties. West Port was a little bit removed, the pubs that bit less busy and that bit closer to the Art College, so hipsters and craft beer. Well, they were before the pandemic. Who knew what the new normal would be?

Three doors, all open. The kitchen was being photographed, but it was as spartan as the living room. A giant wooden bed filled a small bedroom and that took two CSIs.

Cullen walked over to huddle by the bathroom door, which was partially hidden by a bookshelf.

DC Paul "Elvis" Gordon swung around. 'Boss.' His big lamb chop sideburns were visible through his mask. He looked like he could just fall asleep there and then. Like he always looked. 'May the fourth be with you.'

Cullen winced. 'Star Wars day.'

'Damn right. Got the original editions lined up on VHS to watch with the boy.'

Cullen checked his watch. 'Elvis, you won't get off until past midnight.'

'Didn't say today. Tomorrow, maybe. Or the weekend.' Elvis stepped aside to let Cullen see inside.

A claw foot bath sat in the middle of a tiled bathroom. The walls, floor and ceiling were like a giant chessboard. Maybe you could play three-dimensional chess in here, the kind that Police Scotland's office politics excelled at. Or at least, the kind that the senior officers thought they did.

'Downstairs neighbour called it in.' Elvis tapped a foot at the floor like he wanted Cullen to know he knew which way was up and which was down. 'Water running down through his ceiling, had to shut the shop early. Supposed to be open till midnight, but nope. Nine o'clock it was.'

'Getting a statement from him?'

'Aye, sir, but I'm not the DS here.' Elvis frowned. 'Am I?'

'No, Elvis, you're not.' Cullen looked behind him, but there was no sign of the big lump. 'Luke was just behind me.'

'Right, right.'

A CSI swooshed out of the room and Cullen eased in.

Three SOCOs were dusting, one cataloguing, one photographing.

The victim was lying in the bath, feet pressed against the tap end, arms draped over the side. Head tilted forward, blood pouring out of a wound on his left temple and dyeing the tub red like something from a gothic horror.

But it was a flat in Edinburgh. In 2021.

No spooky shit, someone had killed this man.

Cullen looked around the CSIs for anyone he recognised. 'Is he the homeowner? Tenant? Just some random guy?'

Elvis laughed. He was pointing to the red water at the victim's penis. 'Some random guy with a big—'

'*Constable.*' Cullen grabbed his arm and dragged him back out. 'Can you please act like a professional for once?'

Elvis nodded, but he was struggling to keep a straight face. 'Sorry, sir, it won't happen again.'

'It better not, because I'm doing you a favour here. I could put you back to CCTV duty. You wanted more active investigation experience. Here it is, don't act like your old mate.'

Elvis's second nod was much more convincing. 'Sure thing, sir.'

Cullen pointed to the entrance. 'I want you to manage the door-to-door with Si Buxton and Eva Law. You've done it yourself tonnes of times, so this is your chance to show me you can manage it.'

'Of course.'

'First, though, we need to identify him.' Cullen gestured around the place. No sign of any clothes, phone, wallet. 'Find out who he is. If he lives here or whatever.'

'Boss.' Elvis trudged off to the flat door, with a bit of purpose in his stride. Maybe.

Cullen had another look at the crowded bathroom. Aye, this was going to be a right bugger of a case.

Another figure entered the flat. Shepherd, stretching his

crime scene suit with his bear-like frame. 'Sorry, Scott, got held back. Sister called and I couldn't get her off the phone.'

'Don't sweat it.' Cullen was though, his shirt soaking like the bathroom floor.

Actually...

Cullen walked back through. The bathroom floor was sailing, as his mother would say, the tiles covered in water.

But it was clear, without blood.

So, he'd run a bath and someone had attacked him. Thrashed around, spilled the water. Leaked down to the shop below.

Curious.

'Keep away from the toilet, Scott.' James Anderson's goatee beard was still visible through his mask and goggles. The chief Crime Scene Investigator and someone Cullen hadn't managed to persuade the powers that be to move off to Glasgow or, worse, Dundee. 'Don't want you boaking in it again.'

'That was almost ten years ago...'

'Feels just like yesterday.'

Didn't it just. 'Any idea who he is?'

'Nope. His clothes were by the bath but no ID.'

'You going to scan his prints, then?'

'What did your last slave die of?' Anderson held up an evidence bag. 'We did find a shitload of cocaine. Twenty grams in his jeans.'

Cullen exhaled slowly. 'That's a lot.'

Anderson sighed. 'Aye, enough to deal.'

A drug dealer in a bath. This just got weirder.

'Any idea how he died?'

Another suited figure stood up, his joints and ligaments cracking like he was popping bubble wrap. 'Ah, young Skywalker.' Professor James Deeley. 'How goes it?'

'Don't feel so young anymore and I've had enough Star Wars this evening to last a lifetime, so if—'

'Ah, yes, I was saying to young DC Gordon about how today is the—'

'Aye, aye, I get it.' Cullen held his gaze. 'So, how—'

'Keep thinking that laddie needs a nickname.' Deeley was frowning like Elvis didn't already have one. 'He's a lot like a young Harrison Ford, so Han Solo seems appropriate.'

Anderson grinned. 'Hand solo, more like.'

Deeley laughed. 'Maybe.'

Cullen was frowning. 'You do know we call him Elvis, right?'

Deeley roared with laughter. 'That's *brilliant!*'

Cullen waited for it to subside, but it seemed to take longer than forever. 'So. How did he die?'

'Well.' Deeley crouched back down, resting his gloved hands on the side of the bath, then ran a finger along the victim's temple. 'I'd say from the wound, that he was attacked, knocked out, and then drowned.'

'That order?'

'Aye. Blunt force trauma to the head occurred while he was alive.' Deeley was frowning. 'We can't find anything in this place that could've done it. Place is ultra-minimalist, so everything's in drawers or cupboards. Put it this way, nothing's dripping with blood.'

'He didn't bang his head on the edge of the bath?'

'Nope. Someone's done this to him.'

So, a murder case.

'You think the attacker took the weapon with them?'

'Stands to reason.'

Anderson looked over. 'We've got a wee trail of blood running outside.'

Cullen nodded slowly. 'When did he die?'

'Hard to say, but...' Deeley clicked his fingers a few times, the gloves dulling any sound. 'I'm guessing he got into the bath when it was cold.'

'Cold?'

'I could bore you with the details, baby, but I won't.' Deeley winched himself back up. 'Ice baths are big in exercise circles these days. Thank the Germans. Supposed to cut inflammation way better than an ibuprofen or what have you, and it doesn't artificially thin the blood.' He ran his fingers down the victim's torso. 'He's quite fit, isn't he?'

'Stands to reason, then.'

Anderson pointed into the corner of the room. 'And we found a wee hole in the grout. Easy avoided most of the time, but if someone attacks you, you thrash around, spill water everywhere, and it leaks downstairs.'

Deeley clapped Cullen's shoulder. 'So, to answer your question, it's maybe an hour since the laddie died.'

CULLEN DUMPED his crime scene suit into the discard pile, the cool air making the sweat on his forehead tingle. Certainly brought his body temperature down being outside. It might say May on the calendar, but it felt like February. Especially with that Arctic blast shooting along West Port.

And there was no sign of Elvis. Great.

Down the street, DC Simon Buxton was talking to a woman who was standing at least four metres away from him. Mask on and wearing one of those visors. 'Thank you.' She turned and walked off up the street.

Buxton gazed after her, shaking his head. 'Some people just don't get it.' At least, that's what it sounded like. 'Anyway.' He looked around at Cullen. 'Not seen you in a while, sir.'

Cullen smiled. 'Don't call me that, Si. Makes me sound like an arsehole.'

'You are an arsehole.' Buxton grinned wide, all lopsided. His false teeth fell out, leaving a six-tooth-wide gap at the front.

'Jethuth Chritht!' He managed to catch them close to the ground.

'You okay, mate?'

'Do I look okay?' He slammed the set back into his mouth and adjusted it. 'These don't exactly fit and the dentists are playing silly buggers with money.' He pressed the side and something clicked into place. 'Be August before I get an appointment.'

'You could go private?'

'Not made of money, mate.'

Cullen didn't know what else to say. 'Seen Elvis?'

'He's been getting his arms around the door-to-door. His words, not mine. Delusions of grandeur, that geezer.'

Cullen looked around the street, then back upstairs. 'Where would he be, then?'

'Him and Eva went into the shop.'

Cullen peered inside through the murky glass and there they were, by the till. Masked up and talking to an irate owner.

Elvis glanced out, then back. His eyes bulged and he walked over to the door. Mask off before he was outside. 'Got something for you, sir.'

'Elvis, I keep telling everyone. If it's just you and me, you call me "Scott". Not sir.'

'Right, sorry. Aye, so it's not the victim's flat.'

'Go on?'

'Well it's owned by a woman. Victim's male. Stands to reason.'

'And that's it?'

'Eh, no.' Elvis cleared his throat. 'Alison Wilson. Lives in London, but it's rented out via an agency.' He thumbed behind him. 'My mate Farooq in there has a number for her and Eva's trying to get hold of her.'

'Make that your priority, okay? We need to find out who she was renting it to.'

'Sure thing.'

'DS Caldwell is heading out soon. She'll take over.'

Elvis winced and his shoulders sagged, struggling to hide his disappointment. 'Awesome.'

Cullen just knew he was going to have to spend another hour listening to Elvis's woes again at his next appraisal. How he never got any opportunities. How he was always just sidelined by anything.

The door tinkled and Eva Law stepped out, tugging at her black mask that seemed to swallow her entire head. Her hair had softened to its natural pale red colour and her bright blue eyes shone like headlights at Cullen. 'Sir.' She smiled wide, baring her teeth. 'The shop owner saw the tenant speaking to a man outside the pub down the road.'

'The tenant?' Cullen frowned. 'Male or female?'

'Female.' Eva scowled at Elvis. 'You did tell him, didn't you?'

'Tell him what?'

She shook her head. 'Christ, Elvis, he *told* us it was a woman who rented it. Christ.'

The joys of managing a team. And trying to stop them smacking the shite out of each other.

'Okay, okay.' Cullen stepped between them. The stairwell door opened and Shepherd stepped out, tearing off his mask. 'Good work, Elvis. Eva.' He focused on Shepherd. 'Luke, can you take someone and go speak to the bar staff?'

4

SHEPHERD

'Sarge, I just don't know.' DC Eva Law knocked on the window and cupped her hands on the glass to get a look inside the pub. The Debonair, one of those Edinburgh pubs that definitely didn't match its name. A grotty turn-of-the-century thing that specialised in alcopops, quiz machines and fighting. 'Half the time Elvis thinks he should be a DCI, the other half he's happy to coast as a DC. He's been doing it ten years, right?'

Shepherd took a deep breath, long enough to remember hiring DC Paul Gordon onto his team. Long enough for Elvis to be in exactly the same place after Shepherd had spent his five-year tenure in Professional Standards and Ethics. Long enough for him to get married, have kids and run a craft beer podcast. But not enough to buck his ideas up. 'Thanks for raising your concerns, Constable.'

She thumped the glass again. 'That's it?'

'It'd be unprofessional of me to say anything else, Eva.'

She raised an eyebrow. 'Unprofessional Standards and Pathetics, right?'

Shepherd just folded his arms. 'I'll ignore that comment.'

The lights flashed on and a woman teetered into the middle of the bar. Dressed like a Bavarian wench, even though Oktoberfest was several months and a thousand-odd miles away. She shook her head at them and mouthed, 'We're closed.'

Shepherd unfolded his warrant card and gave her the same stern look that had opened so many doors over the years.

She winced and trudged over, head hanging low, then hauled it open. 'Shite.' She shut it, put her mask on and opened it again. 'Sorry, force of habit. What's up?'

Shepherd was careful to keep at least three metres away from her. And he hadn't thought it all through. His head was full of Brian Bain and his vendetta against Scott Cullen. 'We gather there was a woman talking to a man outside earlier?'

'Do I know you?'

The way she was looking at him sent a shiver up Shepherd's arm. It took him a few seconds but he got there in the end. 'Becky?'

'It's Luke, isn't it?'

'Aye. DS Shepherd. How've you been?'

Becky shrugged. 'Staying clean.'

'That's good to hear.' Shepherd was crunching his teeth like breath mints. 'We eventually caught Kenny Falconer.'

'So I gather.' She didn't seem to care that her actions resulted in him escaping justice. In others being injured and killed. Even if she was the victim, she'd lied and her whole testimony was unusable. 'Heard he's not well?'

'Didn't know that.' Shepherd smiled at her. 'Anyway, did you see anyone out here earlier?'

Becky sighed. 'Listen, I'm trying to clean the place up before opening tomorrow morning. It's mental just now. You'd think people would just keep on drinking at home, but they're all desperate to drink in pubs. And the Deb attracts its share of nutters.'

'More than.'

'True.' Becky ran a hand through her hair. 'Okay, so there was a guy hanging around outside. We'd shut for the night, right? This curfew? But he was sitting there, drinking a bottle of red I was just about to tidy up.' She waved behind them.

The seating area spilled to the edge of the pavement. Would be a challenge to get a pram or buggy past, though nobody in their right mind would venture that close to the Deb's drinkers.

Eva started rooting around in the area by the table, which still had an empty bottle of red and a splash of wine in a glass.

'Then he got chatting to Nina.'

Shepherd focused on Becky. 'You work with Nina?'

'She's my boss, aye.'

'Was he hitting on her?'

'Well, they went off somewhere.'

'To have sex?'

Becky shrugged.

'That kind of thing happen a lot?'

'Not a lot. Nina's not like some of the others.'

Shepherd could explore that further, but he didn't. 'Any idea who this man was?'

'Nope.' Becky adjusted her mask, letting her ears flop out a bit. 'Why are you asking?'

'We're investigating a suspicious death at a flat above Farooq's. You know anything about that?'

'No!'

Shepherd gave her a pause. 'Sure about that?'

'Come on, Luke. I'd tell you if I knew anything.'

'We've got previous, Becky.' But he wasn't going to press her. 'We need to speak to Nina. You know her address?'

'You sure I can just give you that?'

'Becky, there are two police officers here. Of course you can.'

'Well, it's above Farooq's.'

Bingo.

'Okay. We're concerned about her as a result of this incident and we need to verify her welfare. We need to find her, urgently. You got a number?'

'Give me a sec.' She got out her phone with shaking hands and put it to her ear before Shepherd could stop her. 'Just ringing. Sorry.'

'Any idea where she might go?'

Becky shrugged. 'Sorry.' She bit her lip. 'That guy. I've seen him before, but I don't know his name.'

'From the pub?'

'Aye. I've been thinking about it a few times. Nina's not been here that long, but that guy tries it on with all the staff here and half the customers. He's bad news.'

'Sarge?' Eva was popping a wallet into an evidence bag. 'Anderson wanted to say he's got a positive on the prints. Name is Dale Mitchell.'

∽

SWARMS OF COPS around the stairwell entrance. One of those where they'd tried to blend the paintwork in with the downstairs shop's decor, so it was harder to spot.

The door opened and Jimmy Deeley lugged his medicine bag out, then headed towards his Jag, giving his usual scowl.

No sign of Cullen, or of anyone in the team.

Elvis was inside, still chatting to the shop owner. They'd surely got everything out of him. Hadn't they?

And why were they so interested in the fridge?

And Shepherd got it—the fresh food was going to go off and that daft sod was trying to get a little snack.

Honestly...

'Luke.'

Shepherd swivelled around and saw Cullen barrelling towards him, DS Angela Caldwell in his wake.

Pretty much the tallest cop he'd ever met, Angela had

Cullen's measure. Of his three sergeants, she was the one closest to him, though. The one who knew where the bodies were buried. But she was loyal to a literal fault.

'Evening.' Shepherd pointed inside the shop. 'Any idea what DC Gordon is up to?'

Angela took one look, then rolled her eyes. 'I'll sort this out.' She hammered into the shop, heading for Elvis and the shopkeeper like a bowling ball hurtling towards skittles.

Shepherd focused on Cullen, but just saw serenity and control. Maybe Bain was completely in the wrong about him, maybe he was just a good cop. And Bain a bad one. 'You get my text?'

'That I did. Becky Crawford. Christ. Almost forgot about that case.' Cullen folded his arms across his chest, high up. 'A lot's happened to us since then.'

Shepherd covered his flash of anger with a smile. 'Well, you're heading for the top, Scott.'

Cullen laughed. 'Okay, but Dale Mitchell isn't on anyone's radar. Is he?'

'Nope. And he had enough coke on him that he should be. Who would have the juice to move two kilos of coke? That's a major amount.'

Shepherd got that queasy feeling. That might be the coke Hunter was talking about. His morning raid. So someone got wind of it? He needed to look into that. 'Still don't see why anyone would kill him in the bath. I mean, sure, snort a ton of fine Colombian and your heart goes phut. But why attack someone.' He looked up at the flat. 'And why here?'

Cullen raised a hand, as if in apology. 'Buxton got hold of the letting agency. Turns out the tenant is one Nina Robertson.'

Shepherd nodded. 'She works in the bar.' He got that horrible feeling that, aside from whatever else he was up to here, this was going to be one of those cases where some daft sod had spoken to the wrong person in the wrong way. Unless they got lucky, it was going to be tough.

'Got an address for her parents in Longniddry.' Cullen reached into his pocket for his car key and pressed it, getting a flash from a nearby Golf. 'I'll head out there with Caldwell.'

'I thought she was running the door-to-door?'

Cullen grinned. 'Come on, Luke, you've been doing this job for *ages*. You can handle finding who this Dale guy is. Lauren's on her way, so hang around until she gets here, okay?' He walked over to his car and got in.

Shepherd should be with him. Keep an eye on him. If Dale Mitchell was working for who he suspected, Longniddry meant his home turf.

But Shepherd couldn't be on top of Cullen 24/7. He had to let him go sometimes.

The dialling sound rattled out of the window as Cullen raced off towards Lothian Road.

Who was he calling?

5

BAIN

'Come fill up my cup, come fill up my can, come saddle my horses and call out my men!' I glance over at Malky but he's not paying us any attention, certainly not singing along. And it's deafening in here. 'Unhook the west port and let us gae free, for it's up wi' the bonnets o' bonnie Dundee!'

And there she is, shimmering in the evening sky.

Dundee. City of Discovery. Land o' cakes. A big lump on the north of the Tay. Just... A city. In Scotland. That's all you could say about it.

Doing ninety over the Tay Road Bridge, mind, but no bugger's about to catch us. And see going over water? Absolute bastard. Not like this place has a good track record with maritime disasters on its bridges, is it?

I turn the Corries' glorious din down as they start up another round and look over at Malky. 'You still not talking to us?'

He looks out of the window at that big new gallery. A wee scratch at his groin.

I lean over and nudge him. 'Mind—' Almost swerve into the

safety barrier! 'Mind there was that laddie took a header off this bridge a year ago?'

'Nope.'

'Come on, Malky. You don't have to be a knob about it.'

But of course he does, just sits there looking out. Wait! He sighs!

'Come on, I swear it's better taking the A92 than the M90. I keep telling you Perth is—'

'—where your son is. At Her Majesty's pleasure.'

Aye, he's got me on that one.

'It's nothing to do with the route you've taken to Dundee, Brian.' He looks over and he's *raging*. 'It's because you've dragged me up here, after a full day shift working with Craig bloody Hunter.'

'Numero uno on our wee agenda here, Malky boy.'

'On *your* agenda.'

I slow as we near on the water's edge, then batter down onto the road heading towards the train station. Satnav says it's not far, but there's a ton of roadworks and diversions and we're heading towards Coupar bloody Angus. 'So you'd much rather we go after Cullen?'

'It's him. It's all him. That's what this is all about.'

'Still wish you'd get over it. Your lassie fancied him, he knocked her back, end of.'

'It's not that.'

'So what is it?'

Malky shrugs. 'He's just a dickhead.'

'Expending a lot of effort on taking him down, Malky, for him just being a dickhead. Did he do a shite in your Corn Flakes or something?'

'Just hate a bent cop, that's all.'

Better keep quiet here. Cullen's as straight as they come. He *is* just a dickhead.

But Hunter's worse.

'How's the drug squad stuff going, Malky?'

'Weren't you listening back at the pub?'

'I was listening to Hunter, aye. But I want to hear it from you.'

'Nothing to tell.' He gives another wee scratch. 'Just working away.'

'On what, though?'

He sighs as we hurtle through western Dundee. The Perth Road hasn't changed in the fifteen years since I was last here. 'After Dean Vardy, there's been a power vacuum. Someone's filling it. So me and Craig are looking into that.'

'Why you two?'

'Search me. Cullen wanted rid of us? It's connected to a case we both worked? Who knows.'

I take the left into a side street with a dead end.

'You have arrived at your destination.' The Satnav's glowing, but I'll be jiggered if we're at the right place.

I scan the street, tenements on both sides, half the lights on at this late hour. 'This look right to you?'

'It's a street of flats. Why's that wrong?'

'Just feel it in my water, that's all.' Still, I let the belt go and step out into the cold air.

Ah, Dundee.

Sounds of drunk kids shouting in the distance. Students. Poor bastards, their year of watching Zoom lectures while staying in grotty halls of residence. No wonder they're painting the town red. Or tangerine or blue.

Sod it, they're actually a bunch of dicks.

Malky's out and on it, though, pressing the buzzer. His instincts aren't dulled like mine. I'm way off the pace here. A year out of the squad and it's like I'm a normal person. A civvy.

He rings the buzzer again and looks up, calculating the size of the place, how long to the door from the sofa or bed.

Christ, we have left it late.

Still, if this lassie's who we think she is, it'd be worth travelling anywhere, even *England*.

The buzzer rasps. 'Hello?'

'Is that Jennifer?'

'Who's speaking?'

'Name's William Smith. Need to speak to a Jennifer Carnegie?'

The line pauses.

Me and Malky share *that* look—she's onto us.

'Are you Jennifer Carnegie?'

'Why do you ask?'

Malky smiles wide. 'I work for a private investigation company. We gather one Jennifer Carnegie won two hundred thousand pounds on a lottery ticket.'

Click, the line's gone dead.

'Dickhead.' I could strangle him. 'You've totally buggered it.'

'Chillax, dude.' He nods at the door. 'We know that's her.'

'How'd you figure that?'

'Charlie Kidd. He's got back channels up here. And unlike Yvonne Flockhart, he knows how to search without setting off red alerts on the system.'

'Dirty bastard.' I look up and down the street, still with no idea what to do.

A wee cat scurries across the street and pops through a cat flap. Great idea, son. Don't want to be out on a night like this, in a town like this.

The door rattles open and this frail lassie looks out, masked up. Curly hair, a sort of mousy brown but greying. An intense look as she scans me and Malky like we're not who we say we are.

Malky tilts his head to the side. 'It is Jennifer Carnegie, right?'

'That's correct. Listen, my husband's on his way home. And I've called the police.'

Has she buggery.

Malky's all placatory, hands up, head back. 'I'm serious, madam. That's a lot of money to just—'

'Why are you coming here at this time?'

'We tried earlier, but nobody was in.'

She narrows her eyes, but her glare is softening a wee bit. 'How much did you say it was?'

Malky looks down at his phone. 'Two hundred and seventeen thousand, eight hundred and sixty-three pounds.'

'Why do you think it's me?'

'We don't. Me and Archie here are just doing our bit. But our clients have one Jennifer Carnegie receiving a winning lottery ticket from the seventeenth draw. Now, where me and Archie come in, we spoke to some people and we found out who bought the ticket, but they told us it was given to a Jennifer Carnegie as part of her leaving present from Carnoustie High School. Right, Archie?'

Archie. Christ. I give a broad smile. 'That's right, Willie.'

She swallows and her left eye twitches. 'Well, I was there for a brief time in the...' Another twitch. 'I just don't see why you'd be searching for me after all that time.'

Malky smiles. God, he's good at this. 'The twenty-fifth anniversary of the first National Lottery draw was two years ago and they pledged to track down all the outstanding prizewinners. Hence our firm getting involved. The lockdowns were good as we were at a bit of a loose end, as I'm sure you can imagine, so we could do a lot of data gathering ahead of hitting the streets now everything is opening up again.'

'Well, I'm glad you did.' She's practically rubbing her hands here. 'So, how do I get the money?'

'Well, we need the ticket, obviously. Or proof of purchase.'

'That was twenty-seven years ago!'

There's a fire in her, a real spark that could burn this city down. Aye, she's Cullen's type. Likes them a bit edgy, doesn't he?

Malky's back to placating her. 'We've got the proof of purchase. Every terminal logs the numbers. We know it was bought in the Barry Road Spar, served by one G. Roberts. Bought by one Fergus Adamson.'

'God. Fergus Adamson. That's taking me back.'

'Bet it is.' Malky smiles wide again. 'So, we just need to know that you're the Jennifer Carnegie, who taught at Carnoustie High School from 1991 to 1994.'

'I am.'

'But you're Jennifer Lang, is that correct?'

'Correct. I married ten years ago now, but I was born Carnegie.'

Malky looks at us. 'What do you think, Arch?'

'Well, we obviously need evidence.' I rub my moustache but it isn't there anymore, so I just look like a sex pest. 'An old passport, work ID, anything that proves you were the you we're looking for.'

'I don't really have anything.'

'But you worked there, right?'

'Right.' But she's frowning like she's smelling two stinking rats who've driven up from Edinburgh to ask her some daft questions at night.

'Well, we obviously spoke to a few members of staff and pupils there.'

Her eyes go wide like bin lids. 'Pupils?'

'Couple of kids there remember you. Scott Cullen for one.'

'Who are you?' She's shifting her glare between us. 'You don't work for the Lottery, do you?'

'Come on, Jennifer, we just need to know it's you who sexually abused a minor.'

She slaps Malky on the cheek. A real ripper, like she's torn his skin off. 'How dare you!'

I grab her wrist and stop her doing the same to me. 'You let that wee toe rag have sex with you, didn't you?'

'What the hell are you talking about? The police are coming, so I suggest you—'

'No, no, no.' Malky takes over and I see he's got his phone out, but shielding it from her. Smart! 'You had sex with a pupil, didn't you?'

'You disgusting little worm, you think you can come here and ask that?!'

'Come on, admit it. Scott Cullen shagged you, didn't he?'

'That's a confidential matter! The school records were sealed!'

'So it's true?'

'Who told you?'

'Was he good in bed? Did he coerce you?'

'Of course— You can't think I had sex with a twelve year old?'

Malky frowns. 'Twelve? He was sixteen!'

'No, he wasn't!'

'He was proud of it too. Bragged to everyone. Showed the video.'

'I never made a video— HELP!'

This is getting right out of hand. 'Jennifer, we're police officers.'

'GET OFF ME!'

'Seriously, we should just—'

'HEY!' Two pairs of footsteps come rattling down the street, thumping really hard.

I manage to turn my head in time to see this big lump battering into me and sending us flying.

Hit the deck and it hits back, really hard. Tears a lump out of my cheek. Grazes my sidies away.

And Malky scarpers, that long-legged stride of his, and he hops over the wall at the end of the street into the darkness of the park.

Cracking idea, so I roll over and get up, then scoot off after him, but something smashes against my knee and the bugger buckles.

Metal rattles to the ground.

Some twat hit us with a pipe.

Some big lassie grabs my wrists, flips us over and pins me down with her knee. That rattle and that clank. Handcuffs. Too bloody tight too, biting my skin.

'Police.' She leans in to my ear, giving us a taste of her strawberry perfume. 'What's your name?'

'If you're a cop, you should be identifying yourself first, doll.'

'I'm DI Vicky Dodds and you're under arrest.' She pulls us up to my feet and pushes towards the big lump. 'DS MacDonald, please read him his rights.'

6

CULLEN

Time was, Longniddry would've been a tiny little hamlet, just a few houses with that classic inland East Lothian style of pan-tiled roofs and heavy stone, but it had swollen up with sixties and seventies bungalows, filling the space from the train line down to the coastal golf course.

And Nina Robertson's parents lived at the fancier end, in a gated house set back from the road. Two stories but wide, and it almost had two wings.

Caldwell was leaning over to speak into an entrycom, getting no help from Eva Law, who was staring at her phone.

So Cullen pulled up opposite, between the cones of two street lights and got out into the howling wind. Must be fun playing golf near here, half the holes breaking records, the other setting new ones for number of strokes. He kept his distance, focusing on the lights of Fife glowing in the distance across the Forth, just at the point it became the North Sea.

'It's the police, aye.'

Angela stood up to her full height just as the house's front door opened.

She noticed Cullen, then looked at her accomplice. 'Eva, how about you do a recce of the nearby houses?'

'Why me?'

'Well, you're from this area.'

'Garleton's a million miles away.' But she shuffled off like a surly teenager, staring into her phone.

Angela peered through the gate into the garden. 'See how much of an attitude she's got?'

Cullen joined her by the gate. 'Her and Malky are as bad as each other.'

'You hang back on purpose?'

'Always interesting to observe and overhear, isn't it?' Cullen took in the place up close.

A big white building, with trees spaced around the building at exact intervals like socially distanced shoppers waiting to get inside.

A short woman tugged her fluffy white dressing gown around her and padded along a winding path, flanked by sunken spotlights on both sides, and met them at the paved drive by the gates. Stony-faced, no-nonsense. 'Can I see your credentials, please?'

'DS Angela Caldwell.' She held up her warrant card. 'This is DI Cullen.'

He got a good look-over, then she turned back to face Angela. 'So, what's up?'

'Looking for a Nina Robertson. Wondering if you've heard from her recently.'

'Nina?'

'You are Jane Robertson, right?'

'And?'

'And I gather you're Nina's mother. She is your daughter, aye?'

Jane looked away, sniffing hard, then let out a long, slow breath, misting in the night air. 'How did you get this address?'

'She gave it for contact purposes to her letting agency.'

'Is she in Edinburgh?'

Angela nodded, but they hadn't mentioned that fact. Interesting.

'Well, you know more than we do. I've no idea where she is.' Jane looked at them for a few seconds each, then settled on Cullen. 'Why are you after her?'

Cullen raised his hands. 'Just need to find her, that's all.'

'Well, that's rubbish. A DI and a DS turning up at quarter to eleven on a school night? Aye, that'll be shining bright. What's she done?'

All those crime books and TV shows had made everyone an expert. But Cullen wasn't ready to hit her with the truth yet. 'When was the last time you heard from her?'

'About six months ago.' Jane ran a hand down her face. 'Whole thing's a total mess.'

Cullen gave her some space to rustle up the courage. 'What whole thing?'

'Her marriage.' Jane sighed. 'Nina was eighteen when she met him. He's twenty years older than her, but she was in love with him. My daughter's a bonnie lassie, but she's impulsive and will not be told.'

A story Cullen had heard so many times. Kids not meeting parental standards when they started to think for themselves. Helicopter parents struggling with the lack of control when their babies became adults. Aye, he was so glad he'd never gone down that path. Or hadn't yet.

'Five years they were married.' Jane tugged her belt tight and hugged her arms around her sides. 'They had a kid but… It's a mess. She was too young to have kids. Way too young, but she wouldn't bloody listen.' She folded her arms tighter. 'She moved in here for a bit, but it was worse than when she was at school. Constantly fighting. Out in North Berwick all the time. And now she's moved into Edinburgh? Good luck to her.'

'You don't want to see your grandchild?'

'Of course I do, it's just...' She puffed out her cheeks. 'Her husband has him now. Keir.'

'Right and—'

'What's she done?'

'We're investigating a death at her flat in Edinburgh.'

No reaction, like she'd just been told her daughter bought a stamp. 'You think she did it?'

'We're concerned for her safety at this time and she may be able to help us with our enquiries.'

'*Christ.*' But the way she said it, it was like there was a history there. Like this wasn't unexpected.

'Has anything like this happened before?'

Jane shook her head, but she was nibbling at her thumb. Denial and nerves. 'She got into trouble at school. This laddie she was seeing, things got a bit much for him, he broke it off and she wasn't too keen on it. Burnt him with one of those flame things in Chemistry.'

'A Bunsen burner?'

'Right, aye. Minor damage, but she was always at that kind of thing. Then she left school, worked in a couple of pubs in North Berwick. And...' She sighed.

'Okay, Mrs Robertson, we need to find her. Any friends who—?'

'You think she's murdered this lad, don't you?'

Cullen held her gaze, let her scan his eyes. 'It's possible she has, yes. And we need to find her. So any friends or relations she would seek out, I'd appreciate it.'

'Well, Nina was a law unto herself. Force of nature, they call it. She was always glued to her phone, should never have got it for her but all her pals at the school had one. I've no idea who she spoke to five years ago, let alone now.'

Leaving them with just one lead. Cullen gave her a last smile. 'You got an address for her ex?'

7

SHEPHERD

One thing Shepherd could do standing on his head was organise a door-to-door.

Even with Elvis on his team. He was still inside the shop, for no reason.

Christ.

Give him his due, Cullen had cleared out some dead wood over the years, but having that guy still lurking around. Somehow. Clinging on.

Shepherd remembered that case where he ate a ton of counterfeit Snickers bars and let a suspect go. Shepherd wanted him gone, there and then, but was overruled.

He stepped inside and got the *BEEP-BAW*.

Elvis and Farooq, the shopkeeper, looked over and put their hands behind their backs.

Oh aye.

A car blasted up the road and pulled into the space right outside. DCI Ally Davenport got out, waving the thickset uniform away. But this lad wasn't taking any of it. Give him a job and he'd do it until he died.

Shepherd smiled at Elvis, trying to hide his malice. 'I'll catch you later, Elvis.' He left the shop with another *BEEP-BAW*.

DCI Davenport had navigated the outer locus and was looking around for his next victim. His shaved head caught most of the streetlight's glare, but his trademark black suit and black shirt seemed to suck in most of the shine. As he aged, he seemed to get taller and thinner. And he was making a beeline for Shepherd. 'Luke.'

'Boss.'

Davenport winced at that. 'How's the village idiot doing?'

'Fine.' Shepherd looked around, trying to spot any stray ears, but they were still alone, unless the uniform guarding the street had bat ears. No, he had AirPods in, white lines sticking out of his lugs. But probably for not much longer, so Shepherd led Davenport away. 'Cullen's fine. It's Bain we've got to worry about.'

Davenport snarled like he'd sucked a raw lemon. 'He's off the chessboard.'

'He's put himself back on.' Shepherd stepped closer, so close he could smell the cigarette smoke on Davenport's jacket. 'He's found out about *Carnegie*.'

Davenport shut his eyes. 'The teacher Cullen shagged?'

Shepherd winced. 'Right.'

Davenport looked up and down the street, clearly as eager as Shepherd to avoid any stray words hitting open ears. 'How did he find out?'

'Long story and it doesn't matter.' Shepherd gritted his teeth. 'What does matter is that Cullen's in for a world of hurt. And so are we.'

'Why?'

'Because Dundee have that woman in their sights for a child pornography investigation linked to a child grooming ring.'

Davenport grunted. 'I'm aware of that. One of them met a gruesome end last year, right?'

'Right. He wasn't the last piece to topple either. Bent cops were involved. Still are, probably.'

Davenport ran a hand over his head, rasping the stubble. 'So how are we going to play this, Luke?'

For years, Shepherd had been subordinate to Davenport, had risen through the ranks as his right-hand man. When they went their separate ways, they'd lost touch, and now they were reunited in this byzantine new setup, trying to snare some bent cops... It felt strange to see his old boss just seem... lost, like a kid stuck in a maze.

And to be asking Shepherd for help...

Shepherd shrugged. 'Nothing we can do, Ally. I've just got to get on with the day job cover for now.'

'But you need to keep a close eye on Cullen.'

'I'm trying to, Ally, but you know what he's like. A DI should be leading by co-ordination, but he's out in Longniddry speaking to the suspect's mother.'

Davenport winced. 'That's what I suspected. He was promoted too soon, wasn't he?'

'Way too soon. He was an Acting DC not very long ago. Then a DC with an attitude for a long time. Somehow he pretty much skipped being a DS to fill the gaps here.'

'Lot of them to fill.' Davenport sucked on his teeth, like he was braving that bitter lemon again. 'Okay, Luke, here's the deal. Take—'

BEEP-BAW.

'Sarge?' Elvis was striding out of the shop. 'Got a lead on the victim.'

Elvis was powering ahead, while eating his second samosa at the same time. Must be cold and fresh from the fridge, but Shepherd could almost taste the spices in his wake. He glanced back the way as he chewed. 'Farooq's got ten of them going off tonight, so he's giving them away.'

Shepherd could only shake his head.

'Missing my kid's Zoom prom thing, so I've not had my tea.'

Shepherd had some sympathy for the daft sod at last. 'Remind me, what's this lead?'

'Right.' Elvis stopped outside a flat, almost halfway from Farooq's to Lothian Road, the thrum and bustle of the busy street sounding like it was coming back to life after its hibernation. 'You know when you're in Tesco and you see those reprints of American comics?'

'No.'

'Right, well.' Elvis scrunched up his samosa wrapper, pocketed it and got another one out. But he caught Shepherd's glare, so didn't open the packet. 'You know American comics, right? Superman, Batman, Spider-Man, X-Men? Well, they import them here and sell them through specialist shops. The actual thirty-two page comics. Charge like two quid, three quid per book. But some British publishers reprint them, shove three X-Men issues together and charge two quid. Stick them in Tesco or Asda and sell a few. Bargain. Well, Farooq sells them too.'

'And where the hell is this getting us?'

'One of the customers who subscribes to six of them lives here.' Elvis pointed at the Entrycom system, though the plate was sheared from the wall, half the wires hanging out. 'One week, the guy was ill. Doesn't think it was Covid, but his flatmate came down to collect his order. And he wore a T-shirt with DM on it.'

Dale Mitchell. 'Could be Doc Martens.'

'Could be. But he matched the description of Dale Mitchell

and I'm willing to take the risk.' Elvis put his samosa back in his pocket, then pressed the button for flat three.

Amazingly, it worked, giving a louder buzz than Shepherd expected. But the voice was garbled, like it was two cans connected by string.

Elvis pressed the button and leaned on it. 'Police, sir. Can you come to the door?'

Silence, just white noise from the buzzer and the hiss of buses around the corner.

The door thunked open, revealing a short man dressed in a bumblebee costume. The black and orange makeup covered most of his face, but his moustache and thick glasses were enough to distinguish him. His wings were flapping. 'What's up?' West-coast Scotland accent.

Elvis didn't seem thrown by the man's appearance and reached into his pocket. He produced his warrant card and a samosa. 'DC Gordon. This is DS... Eh, DS... DS Shepherd.' He put the card away, his mouth struggling with involuntary laughter. Corpsing, they called it in comedy.

So Shepherd had to step over the dead body. 'Just wondering if a Dale Mitchell lives here?'

Bumblebee nodded. 'I'm Tom. Tom Wallace.'

'We've got some bad news, I'm afraid.'

'Oh?'

'His body was found this evening.'

Tom the Bumblebee gave a shrug. 'Do you want to see his room?' He opened the door wide and stepped aside. 'Can I ask you to please mask up?'

'Sure thing.' Shepherd was first in, tugging those tight laces behind his ears. He was sure he was developing some hardcore scar tissue back there.

The flat was a typical student den. Bikes chained to railings. The pong of several strains of cannabis, even through the mask.

Tom the Bumblebee stepped into the open door to a din of

music. Took Shepherd a few seconds but it was that infernal theme tune. *Charlie the bloody Seahorse*. His niece was obsessed with it for a good six months before she moved on. Now she was deep into K-pop. How kids grew up...

Tom stopped outside a bedroom door and knocked. 'Dale?'

No response, predictably.

Another door opened and someone in a full seahorse costume stepped into the hall, then swivelled around and went back in, slamming the door.

Tom opened Dale's and stepped aside again, pressing himself against the wall. 'There you go.'

Aside from whatever the hell Tom and his friend were up to next door, Dale Mitchell had a standard student bedroom. Single bed pressed against a wall, the white sheets stained a dull grey. Knackered IKEA desk and chair. Laptop open, but blank. TV in the corner, a PlayStation alongside. An ashtray with a half-smoked joint. That Charlie the Seahorse poster where he was toking on a doobie, if they called it that anymore, not that a seahorse could smoke underwater.

And a shelf filled with bags and bags of white powder.

Shepherd gripped Elvis's shoulder. 'Okay, Elvis. Secure this room.'

Elvis looked up from inspecting his pocket. 'What?'

'That's enough cocaine to fuel Hollywood for a month.'

'I don't think many MSPs are—'

'Holly*wood* not Holy*rood*, you daft sod.' He tightened his grip. 'I'm serious. We shut that door, you keep Bumblebee and his Seahorse friend out, I'll get the drugs squad here.'

'Sure thing.' Elvis reached into his pocket again.

'And no bloody eating!' Shepherd stormed through the flat, fumbling with his phone for Davenport's number, then out into the cool air.

That much coke, plus how much Dale Mitchell had on him in that flat?

Aye, Dale Mitchell was a dealer.

And this case was getting messier and messier.

The ringing tone bit into Shepherd's ear.

That much drugs was never good, but Shepherd feared who it was going to be. The word on the street. The name on everyone's lips. The man who he was ultimately investigating, who had any number of bent cops on his payroll.

Keir Thornton.

His phone blasted out his ringing tone.

Bain calling…

Perfect timing.

Shepherd killed his call and accepted Bain's. 'Brian, I'm a bit tied up just now.'

'Not as much as I am!' Bain's voice was a harsh rasp. Sounded like he was inside and in a small room. 'I've been arrested!'

'Slow down. What's happened?'

'Daft bastards in Dundee.'

Shepherd stepped down the street, but kept an eye on the door. 'What the hell are you doing in Dundee?'

'Carnegie.'

Shepherd grabbed his forehead. 'Shite. I told you—'

'She didn't speak much to us and… And well, they arrested us.'

'Us?'

'As in myself, Luke.'

'You're not alone, though, are you?'

'I am.'

'Right. Well. You need to co-operate with them. I'll see if I can pull any strings, but I think you're on your own here.'

'Seriously?'

'Aye. Sorry, Brian, but I've warned you about this kind of thing. Told you not to go up there.'

'Fat lot of use you are, you stupid bastard.'

'I'm on your side. And I've got a big case to work here. Play along, okay? Good luck.' Shepherd ended the call.

Christ.

This operation was barely hanging together without Bain doing that kind of thing.

Getting involved with him was a mistake, but Shepherd couldn't figure out how bad it could get. How big the inevitable explosion was going to be.

Elvis walked out of the door, yawning as he unwrapped another samosa. He looked around and nodded at Shepherd. 'Sarge.'

'I *told* you to guard that room.'

Elvis nodded. 'Got a lock on the door.' He winked. 'And I've got the key.' He bit into his samosa, but Shepherd let him have it. 'The wee fella in the Bumblebee costume doesn't know much about him. Separate leases, so not even mates, but help each other out, kind of deal. Hence getting that Incredible Hulk comic for him. No contacts for his family.'

'Okay, once I can get someone out here, that's your priority. And you're actually good at that kind of thing.'

'Saying I'm not good at this?'

Shepherd didn't answer, instead getting out his phone again. Nothing back from Davenport, but there was an email.

One of his spiders, as he called them. Little flagged searches, so when a bent cop was daft enough to run a PNC check on a person of interest in one of his cases, Shepherd would get notified immediately.

Scott Cullen had run a PNC check for Keir Thornton.

He can't be *that* bent, can he?

8

BAIN

Shepherd...
Honestly, you get into bed with a boy like that to screw someone else, not to end up getting rogered yourself!

And I'm getting absolutely *drilled* here.

Not the first time I've been on this side of the table, and not the first time in Dundee, but it's the first time since they drummed us off the force.

Dicks.

This lassie is cut from steel, I swear. No messing with her. Just business. Hair in a ponytail, eyes narrowed to wee slots. 'Mr Bain, you can't just intimidate members of the public. As a police officer, that kind of behaviour is frowned upon, but you're no longer a serving officer.'

'What's your name again, hen?'

She rolls her eyes at us. Well, I'm getting at her, that's for sure! 'Dodds.'

I know that name...

Can't be, can it?'

I lean over the table and try the charm. Giving her the fabled smile. 'You any relation to Doadie Dodds?'

Bingo. She flinches. 'My father is George Dodds.'

I thrust out a paw. 'Then let me shake your hand.'

She doesn't, but I leave the offer there.

'Mr Bain, a member of the public called the police because two men were hassling her.' She looks around the room. 'Trouble is, we've only got you.'

'And you just happened to be there, aye?'

'You were right around the corner from here!'

I can't look at her now. 'But she's involved in a case of yours, aye? Bet you've got a surveillance operation running on her.'

She nudges her pal. 'Euan, did you see anyone else there?'

'I did, boss.' Euan MacDonald wakes up. Dozy sod. Spent a year in Glasgow with the fanny. Absolute shite of the first water. Always one to sook up to the DI. Makes Cullen look like a saint too, hardcore shagger. Still, he never crossed me. 'A six-foot tall ICI male took a jump over the wall at the end. Subsequent investigations were unable to surface him.'

'Must be the boy who was hassling that lassie, eh?'

MacDonald smirks. 'That was you, Brian.'

'You don't remember me, do you?'

He shrugs. Snide bastard. 'What were you asking her?'

And a wee Shepherd is on my shoulder, repeating his advice to play along. Tell the truth. Hard to tell if he's the angel or the devil, mind.

Bugger it.

I sit back and lean my head against my hands. 'I left the force last year and I've been doing some private investigation work for a mate. Jennifer Lang née Carnegie is a lead in a case.'

'She told us you said she'd won the lottery back in the nineties?'

'And she believed it, but it was just to identify her.'

'And what's this case about?'

I grin at MacDonald. 'Come on, Euan, time you showed me a bit of yours, eh?'

'Brian, you're in it deep here. This is a formal interview. Open up and you'll maybe get out of here. *Maybe*.'

'I'm being open.'

'Come on. The whole truth, Brian.'

Christ. That wee Shepherd keeps nipping at my head. Tell you... 'Okay, so I gather Mrs Lang was involved in child pornography.' I keep my gaze focused squarely on his boss, though. 'Little birdie tells me she's involved in a grooming ring in the Tayside area.'

DI Vicky Dodds goes white as a builder's back on the first sunny day in May. Then as pink as the end of that same day. But she's keeping quiet.

But body language, doll. Didn't your old man teach you anything?

I scratch at my head, could do with a wee shave actually, and sniff. Buying time. Watching their reactions. 'My pal gathers that Mrs Lang, née Carnegie had sex with a schoolboy back in the nineties when she was a teacher.'

'Was she prosecuted?'

'Never got done for it. Covered up. But you know how boys are, eh? At that age, they'll stink their winkies in anything.'

They're sitting there, nodding along to every word.

MacDonald pipes up. 'If they're the victims, boys don't cry. That's the cliché, but it's so true. They suffer in silence. And the suffering can be externalised into addictions. Drink. Drugs. Gambling. Sex.'

I nod along like I care. 'Thing is, it might be another story. Miss Carnegie might've been predated upon by a randy wee sod.'

Vicky's nostrils flare. Her eyes narrow.

'Randy wee sod was called Scott Cullen.'

Dodds's eyes go wide.

'You, eh, may wish to speak to him or Luke Shepherd.'

She stumbles to her feet, then out of the room.

Result!

Always rattle the buggers. ALWAYS.

The door slams and it's just me and MacDonald now. Fancy my chances here, mano y mano. And this lad is barely a boy, let alone a man-o.

'How you enjoying Dundee, Euan?'

He frowns. 'Do I know you?'

'I mean, I've lost weight, shaved the heid, shaved the mouser, but aye. I know you.'

He's scanning us like a wee robot would in a sci-fi film, scouring every nook and cranny. Let's be honest, there are a lot of them. And realisation hits him. Like his boss, his eyes go wide. Still, he stays seated

'Remember now?'

He just nods.

'So, how's Dundee paying off for you?'

'Paying off?'

'Come on, Euan. Your mentor worked for me for a wee bit. Used to go for those coffees with her. But I sat and listened to your moans and complaints. How you were senior officer material but stuck as a DC. Heard you got my job when I was hauled back to Auld Reekie.'

Boy, he's squirming! It's *joyous!* 'I'm not sure what's supposed to pay off?'

'Mind at that Christmas do, I advised you to head through someplace like here. Stick in a couple of years, get the experience. Knew of a few boys heading to the great golf course in the sky in Dundee. Boy like you could clean up. Surprised you're still a DS, though. You must be shite.'

He just sits there, caught between the fidget of panic and the glare of pure rage.

The door batters open and his boss comes back in. Stands

there, hand on hip. 'Just spoke to my boss and we're letting you go, Mr Bain.'

Ah, Luke. You big beautiful bastard!

I stand up and give MacDonald a nod. 'Been a pleasure.' I turn to leave, but she's blocking the door.

Wags a finger in my face. 'We're still investigating this case.'

'Oh, excellent. You need a wee hand?'

'You're to keep away from Jennifer Lang and from Dundee.'

'Oh, but I was just getting started here.'

'No ifs, no buts. This isn't your choice to make now. If you so much as pass within ten miles of Perth or Cupar, you'll be back in here. Understand?'

9
CULLEN

Cullen steered up through the new housing developments drawing North Berwick inland, spreading out from its coastal history. Below, the town twinkled in the night, the bars and restaurants starting to come back to life.

Maybe.

He took the left path towards Berwick Law, the triangular hill guarding the place, and eased along the path. It split at the end, but he took the one marked "Thornton", and pulled up in a parking bay, three spaces separated by half logs, with two occupied.

The huge Tesco was down there, over to the side, with the black emptiness of the North Sea behind some high-end housing estates. Across the Forth, Anstruther or Crail glinted in the darkness, but Cullen couldn't remember which.

He got into the sharp breeze.

Angela parked ahead of the spaces and got out. 'Thanks for leaving room for me.'

Cullen shrugged. 'You snooze, you lose.'

But she wasn't going to do either now as she raced towards the mansion.

Two sprawling storeys that would be more at home in Beverly Hills or Hollywood. White stucco, huge windows and balconies everywhere. So many seating spaces outside, but there'd never be any time warm enough to sit out. Maybe a few days in late Spring.

That wind... Christ.

Angela pressed the buzzer and stepped back. 'Two million.'

'You reckon?' Cullen rasped the stubble on his chin. 'I'd say one point four.'

'It's got the footballer bling. And it's massive.'

'Still, it's in North Berwick.'

'Great golf courses here, Scott.'

The door opened and a man monster stepped out, hugging a baby to his chest. Shoulders as wide as the door frame, with big rugby player muscles. And rugby player head, all scar tissue and cauliflower ears. His hair was a distant memory, but the rimless specs softened his image a bit. 'Can I help you?'

'Police, sir. DS Caldwell.' She held her warrant card out for him. 'This is DI Cullen. Looking for—'

'The world-famous DI Scott Cullen.' He puckered his lips and hugged the baby tighter. 'Well, well.'

Cullen had that burn at the back of his neck. Coming face to face with that fame was always a difficult one. All the dickheads he'd put away over the years meant he'd gained a certain amount of notoriety, earned from column inches. He cleared his throat. 'Looking for Keir Thornton.'

'Well, you've found him. Come on in.' Thornton spun around and marched into his house.

Cullen followed Angela into a massive open plan area, every angle giving some kind of view of North Berwick or the law. At least you could sit in here and not be blown back by the wind.

Thornton perched on a squat sofa and cradled the baby, then put a bottle to his mouth. 'Mind if I feed Keir junior here?'

'Not at all.' Angela sat on the other sofa, at right angles to Thornton's. 'Not named after the Labour leader, I take it?'

'Same source.' Despite his size, Thornton took great tenderness feeding the child. 'My son's named after me, obviously. But me, him and Sir Starmer are all named after Keir Hardie, the first Labour MP.' He looked right at Cullen. 'Come from a long line of trade unionists.'

And the apple had fallen pretty far from the tree.

This kind of place didn't come cheap, so wasn't just a case of turning up and doing the job. No, this was the result of looking after yourself, not after your staff.

'How can I help, guys?'

Cullen motioned for Angela to lead, but she was doing it anyway. She'd settled into the new role pretty quickly.

Angela looked around. 'Nice place you've got here.'

'Well, I've been blessed. A few early business opportunities paid off big time. Gambles, more than anything. And I'm reaping the reward of that, you know? This place is a bit too big for me and wee Keir.' Thornton looked between them, but he was fixated with Cullen. 'I know your old man, Scott.'

Cullen struggled to hide the wince. 'In what context?'

'Done a few deals with him up north. Good business. Could see me buying them out.'

Cullen shrugged. 'Dad would probably welcome it.'

'Shouldn't be so honest, Scott.' Thornton laughed. 'I'll use that information against him.'

'What's your business?'

'Started with road haulage. Probably see a lot of my lorries around the central belt, everything from recycling to transportation. You name it, we get it done.'

'KT Group?'

'Aye, but I've expanded. Big time. Bought up DC Energy in

Carnoustie a couple of years ago. The boy popped his clogs, so it was a distressed asset. Cracking business, mind, and I've grown that and expanded down here. Putting my eggs in many different baskets for wee Keir's future.' Thornton wagged his son's fingers. 'Doing a lot of property development, hence the contact with Cullen senior.'

'Sure I'll pass on my regards next time I see him.'

'He must be proud of you. The man who caught the Schoolbook killer. Almost put Dean Vardy away. Who arrested Kenny Falconer.'

'A few times, aye. Bit keen, are you?'

Thornton laughed. 'I follow the news. Got all those true-crime books. Listen to the podcasts in the office. Fascinating world, man. Could never do what you do. I'm too much of a numbers man. Not a people person.'

'And yet you buy up assets and turn them around?'

'That's a numbers game, Scott. All about the accounts and the bottom line. Helps if you just see people as rows on a spreadsheet.'

'But you need people to do the work for you.'

'Aye, but...' Thornton tore off his glasses and rested them next to the bottle. 'Listen, why are you here?'

'We're investigating a murder in Edinburgh, sir.'

Thornton winced. 'Nina?'

'Why do you assume her?'

'Well, it's just...' He swallowed hard. 'Is it? Is she dead?'

'No, but we need to speak to her as a matter of urgency.'

'Right.' Thornton set the bottle down on the table, then adjusted his glasses. 'What's she done?'

'Are you her ex-husband?'

'For my sins.' Thornton adjusted his son so he was sitting on his lap. 'Divorced two months ago. You know when you just realise it's run its course and you... Well, maybe you don't.'

Angela nodded. 'Been married twice. The first, I divorced him.'

'Right, well, Nina's a troubled woman. Honestly, if I'd known how bad she was, I'd never have gotten involved with her. But...' Thornton sighed, then it turned into a broad smile. 'She gave me this little sod, so it's not a total write-off.'

'Seems like a good kid.'

'The best. Sleeps like a log. If Nina hadn't been so mental, we could've filled this place with kids. But she was and... I haven't seen her for ages.'

'So she hasn't seen your son for ages, either?'

'Correct.'

'How long are we talking?'

'Six months.' Thornton put the glasses back on. 'Half his life, Scott. What kind of woman does that? Bears a child, then leaves him? Doesn't see him for six months?'

'Wasn't you chucking her out, was it?'

'I'd welcome Nina back with open arms.' A flash of rage cut across Thornton's eyes, pulling his lids low. '*She* left *me*.' He sighed, the fire now gone. 'And I had to face the fact that I'm too old for her. Thought we had something, but she was too young to settle down.'

'Sorry to hear that.'

'Are you?' Thornton was grinning. 'So, what's she done?'

Cullen held his gaze. 'We're investigating at death at her home.'

'And you think she did it?'

'She might've.'

The news seemed to hit Thornton like a train. 'You're sure?'

'No, hence me saying "might've".'

The smart-arse words just bounced off Thornton, though. He was frowning at his son. 'Who did she kill?'

'We don't know if she did it, sir, but he was found in her flat in Edinburgh.'

Thornton exhaled slowly. 'So that's where she's living.' He shook his head, then glared at Cullen. 'Tell me his name.' Not a question, an order.

'Dale Mitchell.'

Thornton shut his eyes for a few long seconds, then reopened them. Aye, he knew the name. 'Never heard of him. Was he shagging her?'

'We're at an early stage, sir, and that's not information we'd disclose.'

'Right. But you think she was banging him, right?'

'Where have you been today, sir?'

Thornton grunted. 'Okay, so now you think the ex-husband killed the younger lover?'

'I didn't say anything about his age.'

'No, but I meant younger than me.' Thornton barked out a laugh, which woke up his son. 'Ah, Keirie boy, come here.' He cradled him, taking great care to support his head. 'Listen, I've only dealt with Nina through solicitors. That's it. If she's killed this laddie, that's... Christ. How do I tell him?' He looked down at his son, his forehead creased.

Cullen glanced at Angela, but her nod showed she was thinking the same as him—they weren't going to get anything more out of Thornton. Cullen got up. 'Thanks for your time, sir.'

'Let me know when you find her. And... And if she did this.'

'Will do.' Cullen dropped a business card on the coffee table. 'Call me if she gets in touch.'

'Aye, aye.' But Thornton was obsessed with his son. 'Mind if you show yourselves out?'

Cullen nodded at Angela, then led her across the wooden floor and out into the howling summer wind. 'Well?'

She was charging over the pebbles towards the cars. 'Guy's a creep, but he doesn't know anything about Nina.'

'How's he a creep?'

'Well, he's like forty-seven, forty-eight? Going out with someone young enough to be his daughter. That's creepy.'

'Happens a lot, though.'

'And never the other way around.' Angela opened her car door. 'So, what now?'

10
SHEPHERD

The Incident Room was deadly quiet. First thing tomorrow and it'd be buzzing, but now it was all hands to the street teams.

Which suited Shepherd fine. He held his phone to his ear. 'Vicky, thanks for calling me back.'

'We let him go.'

'Wise move.'

'What's he done?'

'A lot of stuff he shouldn't have. I need to find out what he knows and who he's doing it for. So thanks, I owe you one.'

'Okay, well, it might be sooner than you expect.'

'Always turns out that way. See you.' Shepherd put his phone away and cradled his cup of tea, even though it was way too late.

Not if he wanted any sleep.

Not that he'd get much anyway.

Davenport stepped into his doorway and beckoned him to follow.

Shepherd sank his tea in one go, then entered the office.

'Well, Cullen's on his way back here.' Davenport slurped

from his plastic coffee cup, but he'd be able to down an espresso just before bed and sleep through it, then he smacked his lips together. 'Why the hell was he speaking to Keir Thornton?'

'Hopefully he's a person of interest in the case, Ally, but—'

'—but Cullen really could be bent. Great.' Davenport put his feet up on the desk. 'Our mission against that lot has gone well so far. We've taken out Methven.' He winced. 'Or rather, he took himself out. But we're down to the last few rotten apples. Cullen and Hunter. I thought Cullen was just incompetent. Is he really that bad?'

'Is who that bad?' Cullen stood in the corridor, hands in pockets.

Shepherd had that flurry of fear in his guts. The man he was sent to take down could've overheard everything. The text must've been sent a lot earlier and he'd just assumed…

Careless.

So bloody careless.

Davenport blushed, but he was covering over their indiscretion. He got up and necked his coffee. 'Keir Thornton, Scott. That's who.'

'What's he done?'

'What's he not done? That's the important question.' Davenport stared hard at Cullen. Time was, that look would've flummoxed Shepherd, but nowadays he knew at least seven ways around it. Whether Cullen did was another matter entirely. 'How about you give me an update on your team's activities.'

Cullen seemed to have another way around it. Just snorted. 'Rather hear about Keir Thornton, if it's all the same.'

'Bet you would. But I'm the SIO here, Scott. So please, update me.'

'Right.' Cullen got out his notebook and opened it midway through the pages. 'DS Reid is managing DCs Buxton and Law to ensure we get full coverage at the crime scene. Neighbourhood management.'

'And how's that going?'

'Shite.'

'Shite?'

'Shite, sir.'

'Scott...' Davenport laughed. 'Listen, I'm glad you can be honest with me, but why is it going so badly?'

'Well, it's the nature of the beast. Flat in an area like that, it's all transitory lets. A few Airbnbs, but mostly students or casual renters. Either way, nobody saw anything.'

'Keep them at it, okay? Get them applying some force.'

'Sir, I'm not sure—'

'Scott, please. Shut up.' Davenport waited. 'I need you to listen to my orders and execute them.'

'Sir.' Cullen scribbled something down, but he wasn't making any eye contact.

Shepherd looked over at Davenport, eyebrows raised, trying to signal to him to keep a lid on that kind of bullying.

But Davenport wasn't paying any attention, instead drilling his gaze into Cullen. 'And on the other background work?'

'Well, Elv— DC Gordon is looking for Dale Mitchell's family, but he doesn't seem to exist.'

'Doesn't seem to exist? Eh?'

'That's the bottom line, sir. We can't find a home address for him.'

'But you've got an Edinburgh address?'

'Correct.' Cullen flicked the page. 'While that's going on, we've got to find the tenant to the crime scene. To that effect, DC Caldwell is in North Berwick, asking around about Keir Thornton.'

'And the circle is now squared.' Davenport hopped to his feet then walked over to shut the door. 'Okay, so why the hell were you round at his house?'

'Because Nina Robertson was Nina Thornton until two months ago.'

'I see.' Davenport swept back what little remained of his hair. 'How much do you know about him?'

'A fair amount.' Cullen took the chair between them. 'Thornton's one of those guys who's more than happy to talk about themselves *a lot.*'

'Gather he knows your old man.'

Cullen went wide-eyed. 'I... I...'

Shepherd felt like he'd been winded too. That was something Davenport had been holding back. Bloody typical. They were supposed to be on the same side here, not hiding anything from each other.

Davenport leaned forward. 'You going to deny that, Scott?'

'No, sir, I just didn't know. Until he mentioned it.'

'Sure about that?'

'Sure. Bit of a shock when DS Caldwell and I were there and he revealed it. Dad doesn't exactly talk shop when I see him. And Keir Thornton seems to be operating on a nationwide scale. In competition with my dad's firm. So I suppose it stands to reason they'd know each other.'

'Well.' Davenport chucked his empty plastic cup in the bin. 'Be very careful, Scott.'

'Okay, thanks for your concern, boss. You want to tell me why?'

Davenport sighed. 'Because Thornton's on our radar. A known associate of Dean Vardy.'

Cullen frowned. 'But Vardy's been dead three years.'

'Someone's got to pick up the slack, right?'

Cullen swallowed hard. 'And it's Keir Thornton?'

'What do you think your pal Hunter has been working on over at the drugs squad?'

Cullen shut his notebook and pocketed it. 'I don't know, sir.

I'm not a drug squad officer, so I don't ask. And Craig shouldn't be talking.'

'So he doesn't tell?'

'No. Why don't you keep me and Luke updated on our own case, sir?'

Davenport leaned back against the door. Days gone by, he'd have exploded at that. Instead, he just looked over at the window. 'Maybe tomorrow. How about you lot get to bed, bright and breezy for the morning shift.'

11

BAIN

It's *freezing* out there. Dundee. Hell of a place. Last time I set foot here, I tell you.

I head over to my motor, but something's tugging at my jacket.

Her. Vicky bloody Dodds.

'You going to let me go, or what?'

'I'm thinking "what" is something we should explore.'

'Come on, you either charge me or I walk. That's the deal. You haven't charged me, so I'm walking. Capiche?'

She smirks at us. Cheeky cow.

'Mind that I know your old boy, doll. He's a good lad. Maybe you should get a report on me from that case way back when.'

'Maybe I should.' Hand on her hip now. 'Though I doubt he'd remember an insignificant wee wanker like you.'

Got to hand it to her, that's *brutal*. Makes me pish myself laughing.

Not literally. I mean, that's only happened twice. In the last year.

'Oh, Dode will remember me. Mark my words.'

She grabs my sleeve this time. 'Stay away from Dundee, Brian. Okay?'

'Aye, aye.' I haul my sleeve free and walk away with a cheeky wave.

Where the hell's my car?

Car park's half full, even at this ungodly hour, but there's no sign of the bastard. I mean, I drove it back from up the town to this place.

Didn't I?

Bugger it, I walk over to the edge of the car park, making sure it looks like I know what I'm doing in case she's still watching us. At least until I'm sure she's buggered off inside the station.

Right, now I can look for the bastard thing.

There it is. Didn't drive it back, did I? Forgot I'd plugged it into the charger point down the street. Long drive from Edinburgh, even though the range on this thing could get me to Cornwall.

I open the door as it does its magical unlocking thing.

Bugger me. That useless fud McKeown is crouching between the cars.

'What the hell are *you* doing here?'

'Heard them arresting you.' He's staying put. 'Thought they'd bring you to the station, but didn't think you'd get out so quickly.'

'Get in, you bloody clown.' I sit behind the wheel. Well, the paddle thing. The yoke. Whatever they call it. And I wait for him to ease in. 'Not impressed at you scarpering, Malky.'

'Can you just drive, please?'

'Why?'

'Because I'm a serving cop. I can't be seen here.'

'Christ sake.' I put it in drive and zoom through the car park. Can't get past how fast this wee beastie goes. Love it. 'Still, you're a coward.'

'That's fair comment.' He's down in the footwell, hiding from the big scary lady. 'If I had balls, I wouldn't have come through here with you.'

'Come on, Malky. It's been well worth it.'

'Has it?'

'We spoke to Jennifer Carnegie. She definitely shagged Cullen. Such a prick.'

I try calling Shepherd but he's either bouncing my calls deliberately or accidentally. No way am I talking to an answering machine.

So he gets a text:

Cheers for the help buddy. Let me go, no thanks to you. Your cards are marked

I look up and have to break. Shouldn't text while driving, but some people need telling, don't they?

Malky's shuffled up onto his seat now and is looking over at us. 'So what's the plan?'

'Drive back to Edinburgh.'

'What about the episode?'

Don't need to think about it too much now. 'Sod it, let that episode go out now.'

'What, you think you've got enough?'

'I mean, it's your neck on the line, but it serves my purposes.'

'Sure?'

'Aye, sure. Let's cause absolute havoc.'

Malky's grinning as he gets his phone out. 'That'll be the least of it, Bri. I recorded us as we were speaking to her. She admitted to banging him.' He reached around for his bag and got out his laptop. 'So I'll insert the audio from that as we head south. And then I'll publish it.'

Whatever else happened, Malky got Carnegie to speak tonight. Magic.

He looks over at us. 'So, what happens next?'

'You go back to being a copper, son.'

'And you?'

'Oh, I've got a couple of leads. Trouble is, I'll have to drive back from Edinburgh up to Perth prison to speak to someone about a dog.'

Aye, and the lad I'm speaking to knows a thing or two.

Cullen won't know what's hit him.

12

CULLEN

Cullen was being fondled. Hot breath on his neck, lacy lingerie brushing against his neck. A kiss on his ear, then his jaw, then his chin, then a slow one on his lips.

He opened his eyes a fraction and Evie was in his face, all blurry. She kissed him, deeply, her tongue wrestling with his. He ran his hands over her hips and the curve of her buttocks, then lifted her up so she was on top of him, and he kissed her until he had to break free.

'Someone's awake early.'

'Mmm.' She kissed him again, mouth open wide, running her hands over his chest, tugging at his chest hair until it hurt.

Cullen realised his cock was hard, but not for that reason. 'I'm bursting for a pee.'

'Spoilsport.'

'You try having my waterworks.' He wrestled free of her with a final kiss, then hopped out of bed and padded through their hall. It was light, so not too early. He sat down on the toilet and tried to piss, but his plonker was stuck in that liminal space between ready for action and stopping him wetting the bed.

His phone was charging on the unit in the hallway. The screen lit up with a notification. Aye, he didn't care about that.

Then the bastard thing rang.

Nope, he wasn't going to pee just yet, so he walked over and grabbed it.

Dr Helen Yule calling...

What the hell?

Someone he had been intimate with a long time ago, getting back in touch?

Why now?

Cullen answered it with a frown. 'Hello?'

'Scott? Are you okay?'

'Why wouldn't I be?'

She paused. Sounded like she was outside somewhere, the wind hitting the phone's microphone hard. 'If you want to talk to anyone about it, I'm here for you.'

'Talk about what?'

'Well, that podcast dropped overnight?'

Cullen felt icy fingers clutch at his throat. 'Okay. Thanks. Listen, I'll... I'll be in touch.' He ended the call and sat back down on the toilet seat.

He had a ton of missed calls.

A text from Buxton:

Listen to it.

Shite.

This was going to be bad.

His podcast app had downloaded the latest episode of The Secret Rozzer, the only one he'd subscribed to.

He hovered his thumb over the play button, struggling to actually commit to it. Then he decided to just rip the plaster off.

'Morning, gang.' That robotic voice, one he could almost place, but still so far away. 'Or evening, depends where you are. But where The Secret Rozzer is right now, it's early in the AM. And I'm sitting on a bomb here, my friends. Our mutual friend is going to explode, I swear.' He laughed, like an alarm clock would laugh. 'Our friendly neighbourhood Cullen, he who buggered up several ongoing drugs investigations and still got promoted, twice. He who did nothing while his boss snapped his back. He who shagged six different NHS employees from the same hospital at the same time. Well, we've *finally* tracked her down.'

A long pause. Cullen's bladder lost all control now.

'Who, you ask?' That robot laugh again. 'Well, well. Settle down, because here is a story. So, as a teenager, young Scott was such a shagger he even bedded his school teacher. Thirteen years old. I mean, that takes a lot. I don't think I had my first pube until I was fourteen.' The laugh again. 'And here she is, in an exclusive extract.'

Cullen was clutching the phone so tightly the screen might crack.

The clean studio sound changed to a noisy street. Footsteps and distant cars. Heavy breathing.

'You had sex with a pupil, didn't you?' A male voice, undisguised. Someone Cullen almost recognised.

'How dare you?!' A woman, sounding harassed.

'Come on, admit it. Scott Cullen shagged you, didn't he?'

'That's a confidential matter! The school records were sealed!'

'So it's true?'

'Who told you?'

'Did he coerce you?'

'Of course—' It cut off really quick, like there was more.

'And there you have it.' The robot was back. 'Proof that our friend, DI Scott Cullen, has been bedding women since he could get an erection. Thirteen years old and he's all over his schoolteacher. That's impressive. And proof of his evil, my friends. Proof that evil is something you are just as much as something you do. I've got more. Tons more. But first, a word from our sponsors, WakeyWakey, the energy drink for absolute champs.'

Cullen hit pause and sat back on the seat.

Aye, that was a perfect metaphor for him right now. Pissing in the pan.

Who the hell was The Secret Rozzer?

For such a long time, he'd thought it was Brian Bain. Despite everything that arsehole had done, though, Cullen knew it wasn't him.

But it had to be someone allied to him, not that there were many people left in that particularly septic bucket.

Elvis? Well, Cullen was always on the fence about him. Seemed like a good guy, but he had done that craft beer podcast with Bain for a couple of years. Elvis and the Billy Boy, or something. Maybe he was just an accomplice, the daft sod who couldn't say no and who did all the technical stuff for him. But Elvis could know. Definitely someone to lean on and to get to talk.

There wasn't anyone else. Not really.

Davenport seemed like he wanted to kill Cullen pretty much every day, but if he wanted rid, he'd go to Professional Standards, rather than being extremely unprofessional.

Eva Law…? They'd had a misunderstanding back when they were both DCs, but surely that wasn't it. Was it?

Someone knocked on the door.

It sent Cullen's heart rate racing.

Christ, was it the press?

Oh shite—Rich.

Richard McAlpine, Cullen's old schoolfriend and flatmate. They'd fallen out, over someone Cullen hadn't done. But…

Could he have held that much of a grudge? Hard to say, really. Anything was possible.

Cullen flushed, pulled up his pants and walked over to the spy hole.

Holy shit.

Vicky Dodds was standing there, phone pressed to her ear. Didn't look that much older than when they were at school. Still had that hard look in her eye. Maybe it was even harder now.

Last time he'd seen her was across a conference room, three years ago. And he'd avoided eye contact like a coward.

What the hell was she doing here?

How did she find him?

Why had she found him? Why now?

He reached into the bedroom and grabbed his dressing gown.

Evie popped her head above the covers. 'Who's at the door?'

'An old friend. Back in a sec.' Cullen left her to it and walked over to the entrance. He made sure his belt was secure, not that there was anything Vicky hadn't seen before. Just not in a very long time.

He sucked in a deep breath and opened the door. 'Vicky?'

'Hi, Scott.' She put her phone away. 'Been trying to call you, but you haven't answered.'

He checked his mobile, but it hadn't been ringing. 'Oh, must be an old number. Had to change it a couple of years ago after someone kept prank calling me.' His heart was fluttering. The last thing he needed on top of that podcast was her. Great. Just great. 'So how did you—'

'I found a friend.' Vicky stepped aside.

Sharon McNeill was approaching the door, Cullen's other significant ex. Tall and gaunt, hair dyed platinum, tucked behind her ear. 'Scott.'

It was like A Christmas Carol in here. So many ghosts of Christmas past. His present was through in the bedroom.

Cullen folded his arms. 'What's going on?'

Sharon smiled at him. 'This is where you invite us in, Scott.'

'I... Em. Don't want to?'

'It's about that podcast.'

Cullen felt his gut plunge. 'Right. Give me a sec.' He went back inside. Christ. This was serious. He walked into the bedroom and felt like he could be sick.

Evie was lying on the bed, completely naked. She looked up at him, but her lust soon waned and turned into a frown. 'Jesus, Scott, are you okay?'

'It's...' Cullen swallowed. 'That podcast. They've... Sharon and Vicky are here.'

'Sharon McNeill?'

He nodded.

'Vicky who?'

'Dodds. Long story.' Cullen tossed his gown on the floor and pulled on last night's jeans and T-shirt. 'I need to invite them in.'

'Why?'

'Because someone's trying to ruin my career and they seem to know all about it.' He walked back to the door and opened it. 'In you come.' He locked the door after them and led through to the kitchen. 'Tea? Coffee?'

Vicky was looking around the place like she was thinking of buying it. 'Coffee for me.'

Sharon stayed by the door, checking her phone. 'I'm fine, Scott.'

'Cool.' Cullen filled the kettle and set it to boil, then found the cafetière at the back of a cupboard. 'So, what's going on?'

Sharon eased off her coat and sat at the kitchen table. 'Have you listened to the podcast?'

'Not had the chance.'

'Someone's been looking into your past, Scott.'

'I know.' The coffee grounds were still in the freezer, so he chucked a spoonful in. Then another. 'I did manage to listen to the intro.' He ran a hand across his neck and it felt like it was on fire. 'They...' His throat closed up.

Vicky joined him by the kettle. 'I arrested someone in Dundee last night, Scott. They'd been speaking to Jennifer Lang.'

'Who's she?'

'Well, to me, she's a suspect in a paedophile operation in Dundee. Grooming children, distributing videos, lots of nasty stuff. Possibly people trafficking. She's nowhere near the top of the pile, but we've got enough to put her away.'

'And why does this involve me?'

'Because Jennifer Lang used to be Jennifer Carnegie.'

'Shit.' Felt like he'd been punched in the gut. Had his shoulder wrenched back until it cracked. Hands stuck in a vice and squeezed. 'You're serious?'

'Deadly, Scott. Not sure, but the excerpt they played, I think it was recorded last night.'

'Who did you arrest?'

The kitchen door opened and Evie shuffled in, dressed like she was heading to the running track. 'Ladies.' Her face was stern, eyebrows raised.

Cullen looked right at her, his expression neutral. 'Evie, this is Vicky. You know Sharon. Vicky, Evie.' He tried a smile, but it didn't last long. His head hung low. 'Vicky knows who's trying to ruin me.'

Evie narrowed her eyes at her. 'Who?'

Vicky looked over at Sharon, then at Cullen. 'Brian Bain.'

The kettle rattled to the boil.

Jesus Christ.

'He was in Dundee.'

Evie tipped some water onto the grounds, swirling them

around at the bottom until they bloomed, then filled it up. 'So, let me get this straight. You arrested Bain in Dundee last night?'

Vicky nodded. 'He was hassling Jennifer Lang, who is under twenty-four hour surveillance. She doesn't live far from West Bell Street, so it's an easy operation to run. We spoke to him in an interview, but we had to let him go.'

Cullen got three mugs out of the cupboard. 'Was he alone?'

'No. The other guy got away.'

'Definitely male?'

'Hard to say, in that light and in this day and age.'

Cullen collapsed into the stool next to Sharon. 'That podcast. He can't be behind it.'

Sharon looked around at him. 'Bain's clearly not the Secret Rozzer, Scott, but he's working with him.'

'Why, though?'

'You've pissed off a lot of people in the last ten years.' She brushed a hand across his arm. 'Cops, criminals, friends, colleagues. Could be any of them.'

Cullen blew air up his face. She was right.

Evie put the coffee between them, letting it brew, then put the mugs down. 'This podcast. Can't you find out who does it?'

'I've tried.' Cullen pulled the cafetière towards him but didn't plunge it. 'I looked into it. Got Charlie Kidd in IT to help.' He sighed. 'But it's all anonymous. You'd need them to make a colossal blunder to give away their identity.' He smiled, but it felt forced. 'Given they haven't made that colossal blunder yet, it can't be Bain.'

Vicky sat opposite Cullen. 'How much did you listen to?'

'Of the podcast? Just the intro.'

'So you heard her?'

'Right.'

'And is it true?'

Cullen looked at Evie, the only person he'd confided in about it. The only one who knew the truth about what happened all those years ago. 'I had sex with her, aye.' He shut his eyes and the repressed pain hit his sinuses, like someone was sanding the front of his brain. 'But she was the aggressor. She started it. Hit on me. Then... Okay, I... had sex with her, but I was...' His mouth went dry. 'I was *twelve*.'

Vicky glanced at Sharon, then looked back at Cullen. 'It said thirteen on the podcast.'

Cullen looked around at Vicky. 'So? It happened to me. I was there. She pressured me. Told me it'd be our secret, then kept on at me, told me to keep quiet. Told me I was pathetic, how I was a terrible lover, how I'd never make a woman come.'

Three sighs.

Maybe Cullen wasn't a terrible lover, but he'd loved each of the three women there. With all of his heart. And aye, Sharon had broken his heart and he'd broken Vicky's, but he was in love with Evie. 'It's taken me almost thirty years to get over it.' He clasped Evie's hand. 'Thanks to her.'

Sharon was frowning at him. 'I didn't know.'

'I didn't tell you.' His throat closed up again. 'I was... I couldn't...' He cleared his throat and it felt like a frog jumped out. 'She *raped* me and... It's why I was such a... such a *shagger* when I was younger. Trying to prove I was a man. That I was better than she said.'

Sharon took his other hand and held it. 'I wish you could've talked to me about it.'

All he could do was nod.

Vicky plunged the coffee and poured out three mugs. 'You'll need this, Scott. That revelation wasn't the worst of it.'

Cullen shifted his gaze between them. 'What do you mean?'

'It's not about you.' Sharon shut her eyes. 'That daft twat Craig Hunter was recorded leaking a lot of information about a drugs investigation. The warrant that was to be served this morning to recover two kilos of coke, which suddenly disappeared.'

'Shite.' Cullen held the coffee in his hand, but didn't drink it. 'He was talking about it in the pub last night. Shite.'

Evie pointed at Sharon, then at Vicky. 'Scott, we've got your back on this. All of us. We'll help you get to the bottom of it.'

'Thank you.' The words were a croak. Cullen still didn't know who the Secret Rozzer was.

But he was going to find him and kill him.

13

SHEPHERD

Shepherd kept checking the door for Cullen, but there was no sign of him. He checked his phone, still nothing back from Bain. Quite what the hell he'd been doing in Dundee and how it connected to that podcast was anyone's guess.

But the radio silence didn't feel good.

A text from Cullen flashed up:

Sorry running late can you do briefing? Cheers

Great—left holding the baby again.

The Incident Room was crammed that morning, like the first growth after rain. Or something. Shepherd couldn't figure it out, so took a drink of his coffee and cleared his throat. 'Okay! Gather around!'

The hush died down, all except for Malky McKeown. Took a nudge in the ribs from Lauren Reid to shut him up.

Christ, the good ship Cullen still had a motley crew, didn't it?

'Okay.' Shepherd held up the briefing note. 'Dearly beloved, we are gathered here to...' The usual ripple of laughter licked its way around the room. 'Okay, DI Cullen is otherwise engaged, so you've got to settle with me.' He smiled as the laughter swelled again.

Running these briefings was a breeze.

'Okay, so first up. Lauren, do you want to update us on the street team activities?'

She frowned at him, like he was passing the buck for the whole briefing onto her shoulders. Which he pretty much was doing. 'Okay, well. Cheers for putting me on the spot, Luke.' She shivered and zipped up her fleece. 'We've had people there all night and spoken to someone at every address. A few follow-ups, mainly because a lot of the addresses are multiple tenancies.'

'Bottom line?'

'Bottom line is that nobody's seen anything. Not surprising, given the murder location was an interior bathroom.'

'So nobody saw the victim and the suspect arrive?'

'Incorrect.' Lauren shivered again, despite it being melting in there. 'Two sightings, consistent with the barmaid's statement.'

Shepherd held her gaze. 'Becky. Becky Crawford.'

'Right, right.' A shrug. 'Well, we'll finish up the follow-ups by nine or ten this morning, so I'll look to you for instruction, O Wise One.'

Shepherd grinned. 'Don't look at me, I'm merely the monkey who dances while Cullen grinds the organ.'

Another peal of laughter, but still no sign of him.

So Shepherd focused on Angela Caldwell. Christ, Cullen had a lot of sergeants. 'Angela, you were in North Berwick last night. How about you give us an update?'

'Well, I tried my hardest, Luke, but it's like the town's still locked down. Golf clubs were all closed. Most of them looked like they were gone forever to me. Had a few leads on contacts, but nobody answered the door.' She yawned into her hand. 'It's a bit annoying as I live just down the road, but I'll head out today and see if I can shake anything loose.'

'Probably worth being careful.'

'Why?'

'Well.' Shepherd had stepped on a landmine and he needed to get off it quickly. 'Chain of evidence for starters. And you're hunting down a murderer.'

'I can handle myself.' Angela grinned and was swallowed up by another roar of laughter.

'That's what everyone says. Just be careful, that's all.' Shepherd rubbed his hands together. 'Okay, so we still don't have a location on the suspect. How are we doing on the victim?'

Buxton hid behind a posh coffee cup, sucking it through the lid. 'Struggling, Sarge. Still can't find anything on Dale Mitchell.'

Elvis looked over at him, his mouth hanging open. 'What are you talking about?'

Buxton frowned. 'What's that, Elvis?'

'Well, it's just…' Elvis rubbed at his sideburns. 'Cullen asked *me* to identify him.'

The daft sods had been doing the same job.

Aside from any potential corruption, this level of incompetence was going to drag Cullen down eventually.

'Okay, okay!' Shepherd wrestled through the noise. 'Have you got anywhere with it?'

Elvis nodded. 'Address in Cupar, Fife.'

'Get up there, then. I want his parents briefed by ten o'clock. We need that body identified. All that jazz. And remember there are people grieving, so be sensitive, okay?'

'Thing is, Sarge.' Elvis rubbed his neck. 'Cullen's got me scouring the CCTV for Nina Robertson's movements.'

So while Cullen was doing the job of his sergeant or even a

DC, two of his guys were doubling up. And one of them was doing another job too.

Absolutely hopeless.

Lauren held up a hand. 'Luke, it's fine.' She patted Buxton's arm. 'I'll take it. Me and DC Buxton.'

'Okay, done.' But Shepherd was struggling to hide his displeasure. 'So, has anyone got anything else?'

That time in a briefing where shoes and the inside of coffee cups were the most interesting things in the world.

'Okay, then. Keep your sergeants updated, okay? Dismissed.' Shepherd sat back on the desk he'd been leaning against and let out the mother of all sighs.

He could coast a briefing, but this was someone's murder. Cullen should be here for it. Should be leading. Where the hell was the useless sod?

He got out his phone and spotted a text from Bain, of all people:

Headed home last night, baby. Message received loud and clear. Love you, doll xxx

Cheeky bastard.

'Still got it, Lukey boy.' Davenport was standing in the doorway, hands in pockets.

Cullen was next to him, unshaven and looking like he'd barely slept. Pale skin and red eyes.

Davenport locked eyes with Shepherd. 'My office. Now.'

14

BAIN

The waiting area in Perth Prison is nothing like you'd expect. Feels like I'm applying for a bloody mortgage, not seeing a convicted murderer.

Can't help but look at the next table. Young couple, more tattoos than sense. He's obviously done something very, very naughty, but she can't see it. Christ, maybe she likes it. Kind of deal where he's in here for the rest of his life, while she's sitting there pretending everything's okay and he'll get out while they're still young enough to have a family or a life together. And he's too selfish to let her go. His conjugal visits are way more important to him than her future or happiness.

Poor thing.

The tragedy of the penal system.

Still, it's weird being here on my own, and with this bloody mask on. Last few times I was here, in an official capacity, I was with an underling. Sharon McNeill more often than not, but Cullen once or twice.

Hope that prick's suffering right now.

Thing I keep telling myself is... I'm much, much more dangerous on my own than with a clown like McKeown.

Absolute fanny, running off like that.

Still, credit where it's due, he came good. Couldn't have pulled that episode together on my own, wouldn't have the first idea on where to publish it. And without getting caught. Not to mention getting it out so quickly.

Only downside is I can't *see* how badly Cullen is suffering. All I've got is Malky's word for it. Texted to say he didn't take the briefing this morning. Aye... That's him rattled. On the ropes.

Couldn't happen to a nicer person, could it?

The door opens with a secure beep and a bulky guard waddles through. Only thing that boy's catching is Covid, I tell you.

And there he is. My boy.

Kieron Bain.

Daft, daft sod.

Hate seeing him in here. With all the scum of the Earth, the kind of bastards I put away when it was my place to.

Who am I kidding?

He's exactly like them.

No tats—thank Christ—but he's *built* now. Big arms, chest, back and those pointy muscles at the back of the neck. Whatever they're called. Great idea when you're in here to get yourself absolutely massive. No bastard will try any shite on you!

But seeing his cheek makes my heart ache.

A big black mark there, curving to a point like an iron. But it was a stove that did it. And Cullen could've stopped it, couldn't he?

He sits down and folds his massive arms across his massive chest. 'Dad.'

'Son. How you keeping?'

'How do you think?'

Makes us wince. 'That bad, eh?'

'Worse.'

'You not going to get that fixed?'

Kieron touches his cheek. 'Spoke to the doc. I can't get a skin graft.'

'Can't? Or won't?'

'Well.' His finger runs over the blackened skin. 'It's got me a certain status in here, have to say.'

'Figured as much. Still want to take down the guy who did it.'

'He's not worth it, Dad.'

'Scott Cullen is worth any amount of—'

'It wasn't him, Dad. I keep telling you.'

'But he could've stopped it, son. That's as good as slamming your pus against the Aga's stove top.'

'Dad...' He shakes his head, then looks over at the guard like he wants to get out of here. 'Why are you here? It's not just to see me, is it?'

Kid has a point, eh? 'Son, I want to know what you've got on Cullen.'

'That's it, eh? First time you've visited in a year and it's because of another petty vendetta?' He scrapes his chair back and gets up. 'Nice to see you too, Dad.'

'Kieron, wait.' I grab his arm. 'Please.'

He looks down at us like he's the father and I'm the son. '*You* dumped *me*, Dad. Haven't visited in almost a year. And you're only interested in what I've got to give you on that clown.'

'That's nonsense, son, I want to—'

'No, Dad, it's not. You've got a new life up in the Highlands and a new daughter and—'

'You're my only son, Kieron. I love you.'

He sits down and it's like I've floored him. 'Jesus, Dad.'

'Son, I'm sorry. Listen, I know I've not been the best father. Far from it, but... I figure I can take Cullen down. And if I do, we can see about getting big chunks of your sentence quashed.'

That's got him. He's frowning, like he's trying to reopen the bits of his brain he's shut off, the bits devoted to being a cop. 'You think that'll work?'

'Way I see it, Cullen's as bent as a thirty-seven-pound note. Corrupt as hell. He'll be kicked off the force, maybe even in here with you lot. And when he falls, son, any lawyer worth his, her or their salt will swoop in and get your sentence reduced. Maybe you could be a free man again. Could come up to the Highlands with me.'

'I'm not living in your house, Dad.'

'That's fine. I've got a wee cottage on my land. Half a mile from the main house. You could live there, rent free. Pay you a wage too. Do a bit of gardening for me. Have a great life, walking the glens and the hills.'

He lets out a massive sigh. 'Look, I don't have the info on Cullen myself.'

'Who got it? Alan Irvine?'

'That prick?' The boy snarls at us. 'Wouldn't piss on him if he was burning. But mind how I escaped last year?'

'When you faked having Covid?'

'Didn't fake it. I actually had it. Took ages for my lungs to heal. Added years to my sentence too. That bit I'll struggle to get off with. But, the lad I broke out with was talking to me about how much he had on Cullen. Thing is, he's in here because of Cullen too. But he's not an idiot like me. No, he ran a firm for a while. Drugs, knives, even guns. So he had people on the inside, people who *knew*. And he's got enough to drop the bomb on Cullen.'

Christ, he's got me intrigued now. 'What's this boy's name?'

'Kenjo.'

'Kenjo, eh?'

'You might know him as Kenny Falconer.'

Ah Christ. That wee shite. Christ on a bike. Anyone but him.

'But he's in the prison hospital, Dad. He's got that long Covid. And it's really, really bad.'

∽

THING IS, being ex-Job, I know a few boys. Know the right words, the right phrases, the right people. All of which can get me into places I shouldn't otherwise get into.

Only downside is they need to not discover I'm now ex-Job.

Still, being in the prison infirmary is a first. Impressed even myself. Fifty quid bribe was all it took. Thank the Lord for free-market capitalism, eh?

Still, Kieron wasn't wrong.

Kenjo, Kenny Falconer, whatever you want to call him, the boy is *broken*. Supposed to just be like the 'flu, they all say, even though the actual 'flu kills thousands in this country alone every year. Thing is, when you're done with the 'flu, that's you. This novel coronavirus still isn't done with Kenny Falconer, not after a year of it. Always a skinny wee bastard, but he looks like he's dying. Pale, grey, dull eyes.

I mean, there's some sort of natural justice to it. My boy was a daft sod, got in with the wrong people, but this kid is pure evil. Him not being able to even sit up without rasping for breath... Aye, you could maybe justify that.

'Long Covid's a bastard.' Falconer lies back, staring at the ceiling, angry with the world. 'I was just going about my business. That's all. And... Why do I deserve this?'

After what he's done, he deserves the electric chair. Or the long drop.

'You don't deserve it, Kenny. Nobody does. Least of all you.'

He looks over at us, makes eye contact, then looks away.

'Reason I'm here, son, is I'm going to take Cullen down.'

'Scott Cullen?' His voice is like the old boy's before he

popped his clogs. Harsh, faint, each breath like it's cost a billion quid. 'Why?'

Because I'm a petty prick. You don't cross Brian Bain. *Never cross Brian Bain.* 'Because he's corrupt, son. And if I take him down, it'll maybe quash your conviction.'

He just laughs. Aye, he doesn't have the same faith as my boy. 'Bollocks it will. I'm never getting out of here, pal.'

'Seriously. He was a key witness in your case.'

'No, he was *a* witness. But they got me on several counts of several crimes. I'm inside for the rest of my puff.' He looks over at us with real wisdom and concern. 'Be careful, mate, you don't want to end up in here. Ex-cop like you, might end up in a lot of trouble doing what you seem to be doing. Only good side of feeling this broken is I'm not a sex toy for my cellmate anymore.'

Christ.

This boy used to terrify people. Stabbed sixteen nasty pricks, killed a few of them too. And he's reduced to *this*.

'Trouble's my middle name, Kenny.' I give him a wide grin. 'Well, it's actually William, but hey ho.'

He laughs. He's got the lungs of a ninety-year-old who's smoked sixty a day and worked in an asbestos factory. 'Listen, if you want the scoop on Scott Cullen, I know someone who'd be interested in helping you. Someone with a ton of material himself.'

'Be very interested in speaking to him.'

'He was on the blower this morning.' Kenny reaches over and takes my hand. 'The new boy in Edinburgh. Keir Thornton. Tell him I sent you.'

15

CULLEN

Cullen was last into Davenport's office and wished he could just run off back to their flat and bury himself under the duvet.

Davenport sat behind his desk and picked up his cricket ball, a scarred and torn old thing that he allegedly once hit for six sixes in a single over. 'Okay, so we've got a couple of guests, so I expect you two to be on your best behaviour.'

Sharon and Vicky sat in front of Davenport's desk. Shepherd was by the window.

Cullen stayed by the door. He didn't want to make eye contact with anyone. Outside, a bank of dark clouds rolled over Arthur's Seat, promising rain but maybe it was just going to be one of those windy days in Edinburgh.

Another chuck of the ball. 'And we all know why we're here. The fallout from the latest podcast episode.'

Cullen looked at Vicky and got a warm smile back. Sharon was staring at him. He definitely didn't want to make eye contact with her. He cleared his throat. 'Sir, I'm really sorry for—'

'Shut up, Scott.' Davenport tossed the ball up and caught it with an aggressive swipe through the air. 'We're not here for pity. We're here to do something about this shit show. Okay?'

'Wait a second.' Shepherd turned around to look at him. 'First, I need to know. Is it true?'

Cullen looked right at him. 'It is.'

'You had sex with her?'

'Right, but it's—'

'Luke, Scott. Stop it.' Davenport was shaking his head. 'That's all I need. Okay, so I've got the PR team heading here to help you. They'll nip this in the bud, stop it getting any traction. Good news is the daft sods behind this dropped the episode at the wrong time in the news cycle.'

Cullen felt his heart hammering. 'What's the bad news?'

'Well, it's going to be a case of waiting to see if anyone picks up on it. It's not a cut-and-dried thing. Podcasts are very different from radio. Just because it's released, there's no guarantee anyone will listen to it. But there's also the long tail. Someone could listen to it in a year's time.'

'So we'll never be out of the woods?'

'Correct, Scott. Correct. And it just takes one person to listen to it to gain a lot of intel, eh?' Davenport shook his head. 'Craig Hunter's in deep trouble for leaking the stuff about an active investigation.'

Cullen felt that rage burning in his guts. 'Craig didn't leak anything.'

'No, but someone recorded him talking about a drug lord and the investigation into him. About the warrant. While he didn't name Keir Thornton, it's not far off what's going on.'

Cullen swallowed. 'Keir Thornton?'

'Aye. The person you visited last night.'

'Because his ex-wife is wanted for murder.'

'All the same, Inspector. Thornton's been asking about a Scott Cullen. Only be a matter of time before he's all over that podcast. And the perfect storm of a stupid sod blabbing about a case that intersects with him.' Davenport shifted his gaze around the room, finally settling on Cullen. 'And, like you say, while this shite's kicking off, we're pursuing Thornton's ex-wife, Nina Robertson, as part of a murder investigation. And you set all kinds of bells ringing when you searched.'

Cullen clenched his fists but rested them against the door. 'There's no flag on his file, sir.'

'Doesn't mean you searching doesn't set off silent alarms, does it?'

Cullen was aware of all the eyes on him. 'I've not done anything wrong, sir.'

'Scott, Keir Thornton is bad news. You've been in his house, he'll want to know everything about you. He'll want to harm you.'

'I'm not scared.'

'You should be.'

'I've handled worse. Dean Vardy. Kenny Falconer. Brian Bain.'

Davenport laughed. 'Scott, I'm serious here. Thornton's clever.'

'But he's new on the scene, right? We can play into that.'

'Scott, he's not new. We believe Thornton's company dumped bodies for Vardy.'

Cullen felt it like a frozen knife to the guts. All those names and faces they had on their radar who had mysteriously disappeared. 'You're kidding me.'

'Nope. And now Keir Thornton has taken on Vardy's old businesses. The legit ones. And the drugs squad have been investigating, but sadly it's now common knowledge thanks to that bloody podcast.' Davenport looked like he was going to throttle someone. Probably Craig Hunter. 'Scott, Craig's going to be lucky not to lose his job here.'

'That's... That can't—'

'In the recording, Craig said he threw someone off a roof to kill them. Kenny Falconer. Even if it was a joke, I remember that case ten years ago. Lot of grey area around that incident, ended with Brian bloody Bain covering your arses. Pair of numpties.'

Cullen leaned back against the door. He could swear blind to Davenport that Hunter didn't try to kill Falconer.

But what good would that do?

Screw his own career over.

Shite.

'Now.' Davenport slammed the cricket ball down on the desk. 'This is how we're going to progress things, okay? Luke, you and Vicky here are to investigate the Secret Rozzer podcast. I want that bloody thing taken down. Now. And I want names, addresses, servers, users. All of it.'

Shepherd glanced at Vicky, then back at Davenport. 'On it, sir.'

That gaze drilled into Cullen. 'Scott, you're focusing on the murder case with DI McNeill's help.'

Cullen could only glance at her. 'If you don't mind me asking—'

'I do mind, Scott, but I need someone I can trust. Sharon's the best we've got. There's a suspect still at large here. Someone's been killed and his folks deserve justice. But.' Davenport raised a finger. 'Keir Thornton's ex going missing could be the straw that breaks the camel's back. Could be Dale was killed because he was her lover. If so,' he smacked the ball against the wood again, 'we've got him. So. We need to find Nina Robertson. Get on it.'

They all stood up.

Cullen held the door for them to shuffle out, nodding at each one, then finally at Sharon. 'I'll see you downstairs.'

'Okay.' She smiled and scuttled off after Vicky.

Cullen shut the door and looked over at Davenport. 'What's going to happen to Craig?'

'See what his story is, really. It's out of my hands already. His secondment means he needs a serious debriefing from Drugs, so he'll need to head over to Fettes.'

'I can drive him.'

'No, Scott. You're to have absolutely nothing to do with him, you hear me?'

'Sure thing, sir.'

'I've got someone I can trust on that detail. Malky McKeown. Him and Eva Law.'

16

SHEPHERD

'Depends how deep you want me to go, ken?' Charlie Kidd tossed his ponytail from one shoulder to the other. The forensics office thrummed like a call centre. So much chatter, but with the added clanking and clattering coming from the lab. 'Thing with podcasting is it's decentralised.' Kidd frowned. 'Well, it's centralised in that you need to get onto the Apple Podcasts list, but you host the files yourself. And anyone downloads them from your server.'

Shepherd had been here before with this guy. Many, many times. 'So we need to get into the server that hosts the Secret Rozzer..'

'Aye, that's about the size of it.'

'And you're telling me it's impossible?'

'Not *impossible*, just... very hard.'

Vicky smiled at Kidd. 'I can get my brother to help. He does this job up in Dundee.'

'I'm fine.' Kidd leaned forward, fingers primed over the keyboard. 'It's just going to take a bit of time to unpick a few things. Once I've got it narrowed down to the exact hosting service, I'll need a warrant to get the details out of them.'

'Consider the warrant under way.' Shepherd cracked his knuckles. 'I'll go make a start on it. We'll fill in the details when you get them.'

'Aye, right.' And Kidd was in the zone, tapping away.

Shepherd stared at Vicky. 'You want a coffee?'

She folded her arms. 'No, I'll stay here and make sure he doesn't delete anything.'

Loud enough for Kidd to hear, if he was listening.

Shepherd nodded at Vicky then stepped away from the desk, but close enough that his eagle eyes could still watch what he was up to. Close enough he could shoot over the office and stop him doing anything malicious.

Still nothing from Bain. Maybe something had happened to him?

Vicky finally got the message and joined him. 'What's up?'

'Just wanted to—'

'Sod it. What was that phone call regarding Bain really about?'

'He thinks he's leaking information to me, but I'm investigating him, that's all.'

'Why you?'

'Got mates in the Complaints. They're interested in that podcast.'

'Can they help us?'

'Clearly not, otherwise it wouldn't have broadcast all that stuff.' He nodded over at Kidd. 'What's your take on this?'

She sighed. 'Tech is where a lot of investigations end these days. Lost track of the number of Twitter death threats we've had to investigate over *football*. Time was, my grandad would've alternated between going to Dundee and Dundee United matches, depending on who was at home. Now, it's a cesspit of rivalry. Not quite Old Firm bad, but it's hell when there's a derby on.' She looked down at her fingernails, lacquered and glowing. 'As they get more stupid, sometimes people get smarter too. They learn to cover their tracks.' She smiled. 'I hope whoever the Secret Rozzer is, they're a bit stupid.'

Shepherd narrowed his eyes in Kidd's direction. 'Could it be him?'

'I don't see it. Why?'

'He's being so cautious here. Usually, those nerds would dive headfirst into a bucket of Marmite if it meant they could geek out on some weird shite like this.'

'Don't knock Marmite.'

He laughed. 'There must be a reason.'

'You think he's involved?'

'Let's see how it plays out.'

'Luke, back there in Davenport's office, you seemed to be going a bit hard on Scott.'

'He's a sex addict.'

'No he's not.'

Shepherd just raised his eyebrows. 'You going to defend him?'

'He's had a difficult time, Luke. You know that.'

'Hardly.'

'I'm serious. Scott isn't a sexual predator. He's a victim.'

'He wasn't abused, though.'

'He was.' Shepherd felt a twinge in his neck.

'What do you think happened, Luke?'

He couldn't look at her. 'I gather that Cullen raped a schoolteacher when he was sixteen.'

'That's bollocks, Luke. He was twelve and *she* raped *him*.'

Shepherd tried to swallow it down, but it stuck in his throat. 'How do you know?'

'Because I know Scott. He's a dickhead, aye. But he's not a rapist. He was abused by her when he was twelve. *Twelve*, Luke. That's child abuse. And it's exploitation by a person in authority. Get over your male fantasies of bedding an older women here. Scott is a victim. Would we be even having this discussion if it was a Mr Smith and a twelve-year-old girl? No, he'd have been locked up long ago.' She was looking into the distance. 'And Scott's abuser is on our radar, Luke. She's still doing it. Involved in a criminal conspiracy.'

Jesus Christ. These people…

His mouth was dry. Part of his investigation hinged on that. Ten years ago, Yvonne searched for Jennifer Carnegie. His intel had it as helping Cullen hunt down a rape victim and warn her off.

But it was different. She was searching for his rapist.

How did that play out?

It didn't make sense. Could she have been protecting him?

Shepherd frowned. 'Did he tell you about this?'

'No. And if I'd known…'

'How well do you know Scott?'

Her lips twisted around. 'Better than most.'

'Don't tell me you had a thing with him too?'

'At school.'

'Jesus Christ.'

'Scott is many things, but a rapist? Christ, Luke. He's a good guy.'

A good guy.

He'd heard that so many times. Usually after some monster misbehaved, his mates rallying around. *But he's a good guy.*

'Right, I need a coffee. Keep an eye on Charlie for me.'

'Will do, *Sergeant*.'

Shepherd winced. Sometimes he just plain forgot what rank he was supposed to be. Investigating murders was one thing, but he'd returned to his home turf, investigating bent cops was quite another. 'Back in a sec.'

He found a coffee machine around at the entrance to the IT lab and ordered what passed for a latte.

As it hissed away, he tried to unpick what was happening.

Cullen was pegged as a shagger, so virile at twelve that he shagged his teacher.

Whatever way round that was, he'd had sex with her. And he'd admitted it.

But if what Vicky said was true, that Cullen was the victim of a predator... Jennifer Lang, née Carnegie.

And what if it was Sarah Cullen and Jim Carnegie? Strange how reversing the genders brought clarity...

But she was recorded, her voice attached to a podcast about an Edinburgh cop... Where she admitted having sex with him. To frame The Secret Rozzer's narrative.

Someone had tracked down Jennifer Carnegie and passed it to the podcast.

And his warnings to Bain had fallen on deaf ears.

Malky McKeown and Brian Bain had to be connected to it, but who were they passing information to?

Forget about Charlie Kidd hunting down servers and hosting companies. Forget about warrants. It came down to people. He should be focusing on the people behind it.

He logged into a spare machine. Just a wall behind him so nobody could watch what he was up to, so he used his PS&E super-user credentials to log in, then he got into the back-end of the PNC.

Not even Charlie Kidd could get this deep into the system.

And there it was. In the last two years, six officers had searched for Jennifer Carnegie.

Over the last few months, DI Vicky Dodds had been one of them, plus three on her team. DS Euan MacDonald, DC Stephen Considine, DC Karen Woods.

Three years ago, Superintendent Ogilvie of the North Division branch of Professional Standards and Ethics had searched.

Shepherd should've been made aware of that, but hadn't been. Curious.

The most recent search was by Charlie Kidd.

He hadn't been looking for her. Instead, he'd used his own super-user access to do what Shepherd was doing now. Looking back into the past. And he'd found someone searching for that name.

20th December, 2010.

When Yvonne Flockhart had searched for her. And found her.

Cullen's girlfriend for over three years, now a DS out in West Lothian.

Shepherd had been here before. Knew about this search and didn't know what the hell she was looking for.

But Charlie had got hold of Carnegie's address and current name. That explained Bain showing up in Dundee.

But who were they leaking to? That still...

Was it Charlie himself?

Shepherd got out his phone, logged out of his machine and called her.

'Luke? You okay?'

'Yvonne, need a word.'

'I'm a bit tied up just now, Luke. Sorry.'

'It's about this stuff with Scott.'

She paused. She was driving somewhere, her engine whining as she sped up. 'He told you?'

'I'm helping.'

'Right. What with?'

'Back in 2011, you searched for one Jennifer Carnegie.'

The line went silent. Not even changing gears.

'You still there?'

'I am. I just don't know what to say.'

'Whatever happened, Yvonne, it's common knowledge now. So please talk to me.'

'How much do you know?'

'That Miss Carnegie abused Scott when he was twelve.'

'Right.'

'So it's true?'

'Afraid so. It traumatised him, as you'd expect. Everyone thinks of him as someone who beds women all the time. It's more complicated. He was the victim of abuse at a formative age. And he coped with feelings of inadequacy and the trauma by becoming a sex addict.'

'He told you this?'

'We were drunk. It just came out. The Christmas Party. He was in a state, came in to mine and we got talking.'

And there it was. The truth behind the rumours.

Yvonne had split up from Craig Hunter the next day. The rumour mill spinning out tales about her getting caught having sex with Cullen.

Elvis had been at the centre of that, spreading it.

Christ, there was something in this.

'Why are you asking, Luke?'

'Because I think I'm close to figuring out how the Secret Rozzer got hold of this lead. I'll call you back, Yvonne.' Shepherd ended the call and stood there, trying to formulate a strategy.

Sod it.

He stormed back around to the desk.

Vicky was sitting like she was in school, bored as hell.

'I think I've got it, but we can't be sure.' Kidd looked around at Shepherd.

Shepherd grabbed Charlie by the arm, then hauled him over to the meeting room facing them. He waited for Vicky, then kicked the door shut, making the whole thing shake and rattle.

Kidd stood there, frowning. 'Jesus, what's got up your arse?'

'You have.' Shepherd walked right up to Kidd. 'I want the truth out of you, Charlie. Now.'

'About what?'

'You know.'

'Come on. I'm not psychic.'

'Or are you?'

'Eh?'

'Well, you seem to have an intuitive leap that ended up leaking to a podcast.'

Kidd looked over at the door. Beads of sweat on his forehead. 'Am I under arrest?'

'No, Charlie, not yet. But you're in deep trouble. And it'll be much, much easier if you talk.'

Vicky looked close to losing it. 'What's going on?'

'Charlie here did his own enquiry on historical search records. Back in 2010, DC Yvonne Flockhart did a PNC check on Jennifer Carnegie. Somehow Charlie knew to look for that. Then the Secret Rozzer podcast somehow tracked her down.'

Vicky stared at Charlie. 'This true?'

Kidd shrugged. 'I heard he raped her.'

'*She* raped *him*.'

Kidd's mouth hung open. 'What?'

'She's a sexual abuser, Charlie.' Vicky narrowed her eyes. 'Long history of it. Currently being investigated by my team.'

'What, did she wear a strap-on like that case a few years ago? Cullen probably liked it…'

'Charlie. He was *twelve*.'

'Oh shite.'

'Now, I know this has Brian Bain's fingerprints all over it. But I know he's not the Secret Rozzer. So who is?'

Kidd looked between them, then let out a deep sigh. 'Malky McKeown.'

'No it's not.'

Charlie laughed. 'It is. I helped set up his anonymous server and all his podcasting gear.'

17

BAIN

Swanky gaff this. Big old farm building, one of those grain silo things, but it's been buggered about with and has a big glass office overlooking Haddington.

I mean, there are places I'd rather overlook. The town's nice enough, but it's just a town. Big church and that. But the countryside's much prettier. The Tyne winding its way through the place. Different Tyne from down in Newcastle. At least I think so. Pretty far away if it's the same one.

The office door rattles and this big bastard wanders in, clutching a bottle of smoothie. Proper rugby type, all mass and strength and power. 'Ah, Mr Bain, we meet at last.' Holding out his paw.

Be rude not to shake it. 'Keir Thornton, aye?'

'Depends who's asking.'

Aye, I bet it does. Edinburgh's new crime lord, running some freaky business from a farm up in the Lammermuirs. I bet it does.

He takes a sip. 'Can I get you a tea or a coffee?'

'One of those smoothies would be grand.'

He looks down at his drink and laughs.

This guy's a big fanny. I can totally dominate him. Nothing to fear here. And we're on the same side, if Kenny's words are anything to go by.

I hold my ground. 'I'm serious. Could do with my five a day all in one drink.'

He leans out into the corridor. 'Sandra, can you— Ah, thanks.' He nods at someone and grabs another bottle of smoothie. 'Hope spinach, apple and mango is your speed.'

Is it hell. And I never eat anything green. *Never*. Still, I grab the bottle, tear the lid off and take a big glug of it. Tastes like absolute pish, but I'm committed. Give the boy a big gasp. 'Ah, that's the business.' I screw the lid on and put it down on the table. Tastes like the sort of muck Apinya gives the wee one. Tell you, in my day it was all Coke and lemonade and bottles of ginger. None of this health food lark.

'Now.' Thornton sits behind his massive desk and slurps at his drink through a straw. 'What can I do you for?'

'Mutual friend of ours sent me your way.'

'Aye?'

'Current resident of a rent-free address in Perth.'

He nods slowly. 'Think I know the one. Kenjo's a good lad.'

'So I gather.'

'So what's he been saying about me?'

'Just that you might want to share what you've got on another mutual friend of ours.'

'Scott Cullen, eh?' Thornton puts his smoothie down and crunches back in his office chair. As big a bastard as he is, the chair's even bigger. 'The chap who visited my home last night.'

'Did he now?'

'Indeed. Turns out my ex-wife is wanted for murder.'

Bugger me hard and fast. Didn't see that one coming.

He takes another toot on his smoothie. 'What are you offering me.'

'Offering you?'

'Aye, this is a business transaction, right? Kenjo put us in touch for that very reason.'

Total fanny this boy. Got him rocking on the ropes. 'Well, have you heard of The Secret Rozzer podcast?'

'Big fan of podcasts, as it happens. Listen to them on that bad boy.' He waves over to a fancy-looking stereo. Couple of shiny silver boxes sitting under a record player old enough to play the old boy's 78s that I've still not chucked out. 'When I'm not listening to Led Zep or MC5, that is.'

'Brilliant bands, man.' Are they hell.

'But I've never heard of that one.'

'Well, that podcast has been revealing certain facts about our mutual chum.' I leave a pause that's maybe a wee bit too long and starting to hit the irritating-as-hell range. 'Thought you'd like to know that they've also covered you.'

He slams the smoothie down and green gunk sprays out the straw. 'They *named* me?'

'Not quite. But you're on the radar. A daft cop is now in the shite for revealing all about the investigation into your operation.'

'I'm a legitimate businessman.'

'Keir. Pal. I know what you do.'

'Do you.'

'Used to be a cop.'

He licks his lips. 'You were patted down, so I know you're not wearing a wire.'

'Keir, you don't get what I'm saying here. I'm telling you they're on to you. And I can help you. I'm offering my services as part of a business transaction, or a series of business transactions.'

'Okay. So let's say a transaction involves you finding out what they're investigating me for. What they've got. That could work for me.'

I rub my hands together. 'And what do I get out of it?'

'Enough to take Scott Cullen down?'

'I'd love to get a wee taste of that.'

'I bet you would.'

'So let's see it.'

'You're going to have to trust me.'

Christ's sake. Useless pricks never listen, do they? I'm the one in charge here. Not him.

'Pal.' I lock eyes with him. 'I'm going to have to walk across a fair few bridges I've only recently set fire to, so I need to know it's worth all that heat.'

He sucks down a load of smoothie. 'Believe me, it'll be worth it.'

'Well, I need to *know* and I need to know *now*.'

He stands up and gets out his phone. 'You think you're in control here, don't you?' He looks at us like a lion inspecting a mouse. 'See, you think you've got a choice.' He shrugs. 'Maybe you do.' He sniffs. 'Thing is, I know all about you, Brian. I know where you live.' He taps his phone.

The giant screen above his stereo comes to life, filled with a photo of my house. But it's not a photo, it's a video.

Apinya's hanging out the washing on the line.

Shite. I've buggered up big time.

I swallow and it's like I've eaten a melon whole. 'Don't. Please. Don't.'

'I won't. Unless I have to, Brian. But you're working for me, you understand? This is on my terms.'

How does he know about me?

His mate Kenjo. Kenny Falconer. Figures. Should never have trusted that prick. He knew precisely what he was doing. Knew I'd got too greedy. And I didn't listen to myself.

Shite.

Forgive me, Apinya. This is all my fault.

I get that watermelon down my throat. 'What do you want? Cullen?'

'Oh, he's just the start of it.' Thornton pockets his phone and the screen goes black again. 'You're going to find my ex-wife for me.'

'If Cullen's lot are struggling, I'm not sure how much use I'll be.'

'Well, that's not the priority just now. First, I need to see what this Craig Hunter knows.'

That daft sod. Sitting in my boozer, mouthing off about shite he'd done or shite he was going to do. Another trap I'd fallen into, getting too greedy, letting Malky publish it on that podcast. Almost naming this boy. Christ on a bike, my beef's with Hunter and Cullen, not with Keir Thornton!

Why the hell did I not see what I was doing?

Oh, because I knew how deep in the shite that was going to get Hunter.

I unscrew the lid on my smoothie and the smell of it almost gives us a boak. 'You know Hunter's probably under police interview now for what he said?'

'No, Brian, he's *definitely* under police interview. And I need to know what he's saying to them.' Thornton toasts us with his smoothie bottle. 'I hope for Apinya's sake you're as good as you say you are.'

18

CULLEN

Cullen stood in the mortuary's icy chamber, back under the Cowgate, down in the dank recesses of the city's ancient centre.

Jimmy Deeley was working away, singing a Beach Boys song under his breath, like he wasn't cutting away at the corpse of Dale Mitchell.

Twenty-three years old.

Dead.

'Well, he's been getting high on his own supply.' Deeley was working away inside the skull. 'Kid's young, but he's got the septum of... Well. A massive coke head.' He was frowning. 'And you say he's a student?'

Cullen nodded. 'Postgrad in Philosophy.'

'Well. If a cokehead dies and there's nobody around to see him, does he really die?' Deeley chuckled. 'And being able to pull that is impressive, considering the lad's been tooting enough for a Hollywood producer back in the eighties.'

'That didn't kill him, did it?'

'Have wondered.' Deeley looked up from his incisions. 'Fact he was in the bath made me doubt my earlier assertion.'

Cullen looked over at Sharon and saw the uncertainty he'd seen every day as part of their relationship. Her forehead creasing, her eyes narrowing and hiding under the lids. He looked back at Deeley with a sigh. 'I could ask you why you didn't say anything earlier, but... Look, we've been treating this as a murder.'

'And you're right to. It's just...' Deeley's tongue flashed across his lips. 'Thing is, that amount of cocaine can do funny things to one's ticker. Covers it in plaque.'

Sharon frowned. 'Like on your teeth?'

'Exactly. Same stuff.' Deeley slapped the body's tight flesh. 'Kid like young Dale here, in the prime of his life and fit as a fiddle, but if he'd been snorting as much coke as I suspect, he'll have the heart and arteries of a forty-year-old who lives off crisps and biscuits. Now, if he was off his face, like he seems to have been, and had a hot bath then—'

'You said the water was cold.' Cullen gripped the edge of the table. 'Right?'

'I did, but... When you lot pester us for time of death, it's not exactly an exact science.' Deeley laughed. 'I mean, it *is*, but... Well, it's a lot of guesswork, assumption, calculation and ruling out other possibilities.'

Cullen shared another look with Sharon. 'So what other possibilities are you ruling out?'

'I'd assumed he'd not been in there a while and the water had run cold... That he'd got in there. Thing is, hot baths can cause heart arrhythmia. The state of his ticker, even at his age, could've caused a massive coronary. Well, his blood alcohol levels were very high, but the sheer amount of cocaine racing around his bloodstream would mean it's possible he just couldn't get out of the bath, couldn't get help.'

'We've got sightings of him ninety minutes before it was called in.'

'Have you now?' Deeley carried on, seeming unperturbed. 'And human beings have never lied, have they? Nope, nosiree.'

Cullen could see his point—someone lying about seeing Dale with Nina, just to...

What?

Put her in the frame? It was possible. Keir Thornton seemed to have claws in everything, so maybe their witnesses weren't pure.

Cullen leaned forward, making eye contact. 'How can you prove this?'

'I'm going to open his heart again.'

Sharon ran a hand down her face. 'I need a coffee.'

'Sure. I'll be but a moment. Coffee machine in my office is working again, though I'd avoid the milk, it's lumpier than my lumbar region.'

'Thanks.' Sharon jerked her head towards Deeley's inner sanctum and set off, while the man himself worked away at the corpse.

Cullen followed her through.

She shut the door and let out a deep breath. 'Christ, he doesn't get any easier to deal with, does he?'

'Getting worse with age.' Cullen found the coffee machine and it wasn't fit for human consumption. An old filter job, the jug smeared with dark brown stains he hoped was old coffee. 'I'll pass on that drink, then.' He poured a glass of water from the tap and sank it. 'Always find PMs frustrating.'

'Is that because they're always with Jimmy Deeley?'

'Not always, but probably.'

She smiled at him, but it turned sour. 'Why didn't you tell me?'

'About Deeley?'

'No, Scott, about how you were abused as a child.'

Cullen saw a tent, a campsite. Miss Carnegie. And he *was* a child. Twelve years old.

And afterwards, she made him feel younger. And tiny, like he was a baby again. So small.

He couldn't look at Sharon. Tears were stinging his eyes.

'Hey.' She was stroking his back. 'It's okay.'

'It's not, is it?' The tears sluiced down his cheeks. 'She knew what she was doing. Knew how boys don't cry. And I never did. Until now.' He lost control of his mouth. 'I told Evie, ten years ago. She wanted to help, to arrest Miss Carnegie, but... But I ran away. Blocked her out of my life.'

She hugged him, tighter than she used to. 'It's okay.'

He leaned into it, wrapped his arms around her and just clung on to her.

'Hey, hey. Scott, it's okay.'

He broke free. 'Afterwards, the way she belittled me... It left a scar on me. I just don't get what she got out of it. Why?'

'It's power, Scott. It's always about power. I've been in the Sexual Offences Unit for over seven years now. I've seen it so many times. It's always the same two or three motivations. And it's nothing like you maybe reminded her of someone in her past, that's a myth. Sexual offenders are master profilers. They know their victims. Maybe she figured you wouldn't tell. Perhaps she disliked you or wanted to demonstrate her power over you, to be in control. Scott, it could be just as innocuous as you had the right height, weight and hair colour. But the point is, you didn't get to decide. She did.'

It made perfect sense. But it also made him shiver. Something that had such a profound effect on his life... And there was nothing he could've done to avoid it.

She ran a hand through her hair. 'Listen, Vicky and I have been working that case together. Her from the Dundee end, me from the Sexual Offences Unit. The ring stretches down to the central belt, as I'm sure you can imagine. We've spoken to other victims of Miss Carnegie. She's got a type, Scott. Boys like you were. Twelve years old and younger. And she singles them out, gets them to comply and then confronts them with their own acquiescence. And she casts them aside, where the psychological abuse is at least as bad. And she's got very good at silencing them.'

Cullen couldn't look at her. 'If I'd come forward, those others wouldn't—'

'No, Scott. If you'd come forward, I doubt you'd have got anywhere. An older women with a younger man? It's a lot of boys' fantasies. Maybe a teacher would've believed you, supported you. Your parents definitely would. But the system then was so broken.'

'Right. I know. The reality is horrible, though. It's not the... the sex, though that didn't... Didn't... It's...'

'I know, Scott. I know.' She held his gaze for a few seconds, long enough for the tears to subside. 'Having your dirty laundry aired in public has got to hurt too.'

And it did. Right in his heart, in his guts. Like electricity fizzing up and down his legs and arms. Shame, so much shame. 'That's the worst part.'

'The worst? Really?'

'Everyone knowing, aye.'

She hugged him again. 'Oh, Scott.'

He didn't reciprocate this time, just felt numb to it. 'I hope Vicky and Shepherd find out who's doing that podcast.'

'You think it's Bain?'

'Would put money on it, but he's not that daft. Swore it wasn't him.'

'And you believe him?'

'For the first time in my life, aye. I don't think he's doing it.' Cullen swallowed it all down, all the shame and revulsion and years of guilt. 'You've been working with Vicky for a while now?'

'Since last year, aye.' Sharon exhaled slowly. 'Our paths

crossed on a case and we've been stuck together like that since. She's a good cop.'

'One of the best. Even for a Dundonian.'

'She's from Carnoustie, though.'

'Aye, but it's the same difference. Her family's from there.'

She brushed her hair back behind her ear. 'I didn't know you two were an item at school.'

Cullen refilled his glass and downed it. 'Lived in Carnoustie for a year, after what happened with Miss Carnegie. My mum and dad were good about it, tried to help in any way they could.'

'You told them?'

'God no. But they could tell I wasn't happy. Uprooted us for a bit. Dad was a business manager in the trades. He could work anywhere, so he quit and got a job down there at a plumbing company. But Vicky helped me, in ways she can't understand.' He felt that lump back in his throat. 'But also... She was my first girlfriend. It's probably why I'm a "shagger".' He even did the rabbit ears. 'She liked me, made me feel a bit better about myself. That I wasn't all those things Miss Carnegie said about me.' He swallowed the lump down. 'And you helped me heal.'

'Even with how this ended between us?'

Cullen shrugged. 'Thanks for being so understanding. I needed that.'

The door swung open and Deeley leered inside. 'You two lovebirds should get a room.'

Cullen tried to laugh it off, but nope. It wasn't happening. He walked up to him. 'That's not funny.'

'No.' Deeley stepped back. 'I guess not.' He looked at Sharon. 'Actually, you know what? I'd like to apologise on Bain's behalf for the Butch nickname. I never liked it.'

'So why are you apologising?'

'Because I let him use it in here. If you don't stand up to bullies, they get away with it.'

Sharon pushed past him back into the lab. 'Let's just get on with it, shall we?'

'Right-o.' Deeley gave Cullen a pair of raised eyebrows, then walked over to the corpse. 'Okay, so cause of death wasn't a heart attack, but it was definitely from drowning, aided and abetted by the blunt force trauma to the head. Presence of water in the lungs shows it was attempted drowning. Bathwater, but no soap in there. The blow could've knocked him out, but not killed him. There's no blood spatter on the tiles behind, so it's possible it came during the drowning. But they drowned him and that's what killed him.' He held up a tablet computer. 'High levels of alcohol in his bloodstream, like you on a night out, Scott, would indicate an inability to fend off his attacker. And cocaine, lots of it.'

'And you're a hundred percent sure?'

'Right. That coke's being analysed by Anderson's clowns. Early results are that it's good stuff. *Very* good stuff. You'd normally get markers from talc or rat poison, but this is about eighty percent. Normally, they'd cut it with something to boost their profit. Street stuff would be twenty to thirty, so this is close to the supplier. There's a lot of Colombia's finest in this.'

Sharon was frowning at Cullen. 'How likely is it for a postgraduate student to get Hollywood coke?'

'Not very.' Cullen narrowed his eyes. 'Remember I did a stint on the drugs squad a few years ago? The closest we got was seventy percent, cut with bicarbonate of soda, but that was in some clubs down on George Street. Most of it was twenty, thirty maximum. To get close to a hundred percent, you're giving up like four times street value for personal use.'

Cullen's phone blasted out.

Ange calling...

He walked over to the door. 'Better take this.' He stepped through and answered. 'You okay?'

'As well as can be. Shepherd's just taken Malky McKeown away without my approval.'

Cullen let out a sigh. Some days, he'd just like to get on with solving cases instead of processing stupid shit between his officers. 'He's still with the drugs squad, isn't he?'

'Apparently, he's been farmed back to you. And Davenport knows all about it.'

And that'll be another email in his inbox that he'd get around to reading in 2053. 'Right, I'll sort it out.'

'Wait, there's another thing.' Angela paused. 'Elvis has actually pulled out his finger.'

'Go on?'

'He's found some CCTV from a bank ATM over the road from Nina's flat. Just after the estimated time of death, we've got Nina running off, but Becky was with her.'

Cullen tried to replay events, establish a timeline.

Becky insisted she was in the pub all that time.

Aye, people never lied, did they? Maybe Deeley was right, damn him.

'Okay. Bring her in.'

19

SHEPHERD

One part of the job Shepherd hated was the betrayal. His own, he could cope with, as it was all in the service of the greater good.

But everyone else's sat like a pain in the pit of his stomach.

Shepherd still struggled to process the fact that Malky McKeown was The Secret Rozzer. He'd thought he was a stooge, but what Charlie showed him... He was The Secret Rozzer.

Hiding in plain sight.

Not that Shepherd could find him.

The Incident Room was empty, just the usual cottage industry built up around that sad sack of an admin officer, hidden amongst his group of underlings. Way too heavy to run anything other than a spreadsheet, his hair streaked with grey, his round face a dangerous purple. Running queries against HOLMES, updating actions, creating busy work. Fretting about tedious shit.

Still, Shepherd needed to speak to him.

Just couldn't remember his name. Holding? Holden? Holdsworth? That was it. Bryan? Maybe. Hmm.

'DS Holdsworth, need a word.'

He looked over at Shepherd, then back down at his laptop. 'Well, we're kind of up against it here, so if—'

'Just need to know Malky McKeown's whereabouts. Drugs squad don't know where he is.'

'Because he's been reallocated to DS Caldwell.'

'Right.' Great, just fantastic. 'Well, I'll pick up with her.' Shepherd left the room and powered along the corridor.

And DC Eva Law walked towards him, lugging three packs of printer paper.

Malky McKeown's girlfriend.

His co-conspirator.

Shepherd took the paper off her. 'Need a word, Constable.' He led her down the corridor, trying to act cool. 'You okay?'

'I'm good.' But she was frowning.

He stopped outside the door and held it open. 'In here.'

Vicky Dodds was working at a laptop. She stopped and set it aside. 'Getting anywhere?'

'Not found him.' Shepherd ushered Eva inside the room. 'But she might know.'

Eva looked between them, then at the door. 'What might I know?'

Eva had worked for Shepherd for the last year, since he'd been back in MIT. She seemed good, capable and competent. And yet...

He shut the door and leaned back against it. 'Wondering what your boyfriend is up to.'

'Malky's working for the drug squad.'

'Okay. But I was more interested in The Secret Rozzer.'

'The what?'

'The podcast.'

She laughed. 'A podcast? What the hell are you talking about?'

'Don't mess with me, Eva. Someone's been leaking confidential matters pertaining to ongoing investigations.'

'That'll be Bain.'

'Bain?'

'Brian Bain. Used to be a cop.'

'You sure about that?'

'No, but it's who I'd guess was doing it. He's got it in for Cullen.'

Shepherd looked over at Vicky, but she seemed happy to follow their back and forth. 'Why do you mention his name?'

'Eh?'

'Of all the people in this station, you homed in on the one person who has been explicitly targeted, despite not knowing anything about the podcast.'

'It's nothing to do with me!'

'Eva, you're deep in the shite. We know it's you and Malky.'

'It's not!'

'I don't believe you.' Shepherd stepped forward and slammed a fist on the table. 'I've got evidence that Malky's behind this. And I think you're working with him. And I think Bain's been helping you.'

'No smoke without fire.'

As good as an admission. 'Right, then I'm going to prosecute you for surreptitiously recording police officers. You'll lose your pension, probably face prison.'

Eva went white. 'What?'

'I hate to do this, but it can't just be Cullen and crew who talk in the Cheeky Judge, can it?'

'Why there?'

'I know all about it, Eva. It's owned by Brian Bain. You want to tell us what he's been doing in there?'

'No.'

'Didn't think you did. You going to be a good girl and do it anyway?'

She shook her head.

'It could be worth your while.' That got a twitch from her eyes. 'See, you're deep in it here. And I mean it's above your head. And you're tied to the bottom. Don't sink with them. Help us.'

A sigh erupted from her mouth. 'He's been recording cops in there.'

So Bain was a lying bastard. He'd told Shepherd—*to his face*—that he hadn't.

But then, Shepherd should never have trusted Bain. 'I wonder what else you've got, what you haven't broadcast. Who you've sold that information to.'

She collapsed into a chair. 'I'm sorry.'

'That's not going to cut it. Now, I suggest you talk to us. Open up. And we'll see what we can do. I suspect you're the least involved, right?'

'Okay.' She blew air up her face. 'It's mainly Malky and Bain. Plus a few others. Willie McAllister. Charlie Kidd.' Shepherd caught Vicky's look. 'But Bain's been doing the recording, Malky does the podcast. He chooses what they say.'

'And that's all?'

'I don't do anything but run the Twitter and Instagram accounts.'

'You're still party to it, Eva. You're still in deep trouble.'

Another shrug.

This was too easy. Confront her and she folded.

There had to be more to it than this. Had to be. Maybe Charlie was lying.

'Why are you doing it?'

'Because I hate Scott Cullen.' She shrugged. 'That's it. I just want to see him suffer.'

'What did he ever do to you, Eva?'

Another shrug.

'You've broken the law. You're going to lose your job. Just tell me who you're really working for?'

'Nobody.'

'Is that there's nobody or you don't know?'

'I don't know.'

'Do you know where Malky is right now?'

She shook her head.

'What about Bain?'

'Supposed to meet him in his pub this morning, but he didn't show up. The Cheeky Judge.'

Shepherd leaned forward. 'Right, here's what's going to happen, Eva. You're going to sit here. One of my colleagues will come along and process you. I advise you give them everything. What you've done. Who else is involved. Who's not. And any intelligence on who else might be.'

'Okay.'

He held out a hand. 'I need your phone.'

'Okay.' She reached into her pocket and got it out. 'I really am sorry.'

'Well, thank you. I'll pass on your apologies to Scott.'

'No way.'

'Eva, he's the victim of sexual abuse. And you've been discussing him in public.'

'No way, he's a rapist.'

'Eva, he was sexually abused when he was twelve.'

Her head hung low. 'Jesus.'

Shepherd left the room and gestured for Vicky to follow him. 'Can you stay here with her? DI Muir will be along to process her soon.'

'Who's he?'

'A colleague.'

'Well, why can't *you* stay here?'

'Because I'm giving you an order, Vicky.'

She laughed. 'Luke, you're a DS, I'm a DI.'

'I could argue the toss and say you've been in that role less than a year, Vicky, but here's the clincher.' He reached into his pocket for his real warrant card. 'DCI Luke Shepherd. Professional Standards and Ethics.'

∾

ANOTHER PART of the job Shepherd hated—dealing with people who'd been over-promoted.

Angela Caldwell had been an adequate constable, a decent detective, but she was nobody's sergeant. Nobody except for Scott Cullen. And Shepherd was having to deal with her constant drama.

She wasn't letting him get away. 'Okay, so I've just spoken to Scott. He wants you to call him.'

Shepherd looked over the road, where a few officers huddled around, drinking cups of tea. Elvis was showing them something on his phone and Malky McKeown was laughing loudest.

The arsehole was up to his armpits in excrement and it was still filling up. Leaking police secrets on a podcast.

Shepherd needed him in an interview room, needed him speaking. 'I'll pick up Scott back at the station, thanks very much.' He set off across the road towards them.

Angela blocked his path. 'You try and take him, and I'll smash your face in.'

Shepherd looked her up and down. He could tell she meant it. Why did it always have to come down to threats of violence? He gave her a smile. 'I just need a word with him at the station, then—'

'Nope. Nope, nope, nope.' She shook her head. 'You're swanning around playing your games, Luke, when some of us are trying to catch a murderer.' She waved a hand down the street at the Debonair bar, already doing a brisk trade in early morning alcoholism. 'I've got two guys self-isolating today because of their kids, so I need Malky to help out.'

The last person anyone needed. 'Angela, I'm sorry, but I need time with Malky.'

'What's he done?'

'I can't tell you.'

'So you're just being a dickhead, then? Right.' She laughed. 'I'll suggest you *stop* being a dickhead and let others do their jobs.'

Shepherd tried to play through the equation in his head. He could fight fire with fire here, but was that the right move? He had Malky McKeown in his sights. Get him in the car. Just a short drive to the station and he could get him talking. Admitting everything he'd done. Who he was working for.

But she was going to fight him. Causing a scene. Spooking McKeown. Maybe letting him alert who he was with.

Shepherd sighed. 'What do you need him to do?'

'DI Cullen's asked me to escort Becky Crawford to custody. I need Malky to do that.'

Becky...

Shepherd didn't like her being in the line of fire here. 'What's she done?'

'Lied. Repeatedly.'

Just then, Hunter stepped out of the Debonair. He looked seriously hungover—dark rings under his eyes, that slope to his big shoulders—as he led Becky Crawford over to them. 'Sarge, she's coming of her own volition.'

How the hell was he out on the streets? He should be in a police cell after what he was caught saying.

'Good.' Angela smiled at Shepherd. 'So, can you and DC McKeown take her back to St Leonard's?'

'Will do.' Hunter waved at Malky and some silent communication passed between them. 'Let's go.'

Hunter and McKeown walked her over to a battered pool

Volvo. Hard to tell its original colour, probably a pale green, but it could also be a dark grey. The mud caked to the side didn't help.

All Shepherd needed to do was let them get back to the station, then pounce. So he backed down, palms raised. 'On you go, Angela.'

'Just like that?'

'Sorry, I haven't had my second coffee of the day.' Shepherd walked over to Hunter and separated them. 'Craig, make sure you get them back to the station.'

'What's going on?'

Shepherd whispered, 'He's the Secret Rozzer.'

Hunter was good, though. A microsecond of surprise covered over with a laugh. 'Not that I've heard.'

'I'll see you back at the station.' Shepherd walked off down the street, past the Debonair, and got in his car.

Angela was glaring at him, clearly not happy about his behaviour. She'd be on the phone to Cullen as soon as he left.

The Volvo swung around and headed back to the Grassmarket.

Shepherd eased off, following them towards the station.

An easy run, just a couple of traffic hotspots that were probably okay at this time of day. Then he'd have Malky at the station and Cullen would have Becky. And all would be right in the world.

The Grassmarket was quiet for this time of day, but then everywhere was. Would take months to get back to even last autumn's levels, let alone pre-pandemic. If it ever did.

Malky hung his arm out of the driver's window. Snide wee bastard. Recording people like Craig Hunter and broadcasting police secrets. Maybe nobody listened to that podcast, but maybe hundreds did. Goading Charlie Kidd to leak confidential information. Aye, he was deep in the shit. He'd lose his job, possibly face jail time. Whatever he'd gained from the transaction, Shepherd couldn't imagine anything that was worth it.

Maybe Malky had something on him. Or maybe it was just pettiness.

Shepherd passed Bannerman's and the new Sainsbury's Local, right down in the bowels of the Cowgate, where the sunlight barely ventured. Traffic was slow, but he could see the Volvo two cars ahead, slowing as they approached the lights at the junction with Holyrood Road and the Pleasance.

A delivery lorry pulled in opposite the Volvo, hazards flashing away. The driver and the passenger hopped out.

They were wearing balaclavas.

Shite.

Shepherd killed the engine and got out onto the street.

They had opened both doors and were aiming pistols inside the car.

Shepherd hid behind a bin, peering around it.

McKeown was getting out, hands on his head.

Whoever Malky was working for, whoever he was doing this podcast for, they were connected. They didn't want him out on the street, potentially shooting his mouth off under police interview.

They were taking him off the board now.

The car was empty. Christ, they'd already got Becky!

Shepherd darted forward, his knees creaking as he kept low to the ground, then raced forward and rugby tackled the goon with McKeown. The gun slid along the pavement.

Shepherd grabbed his wrist and pinned him down. 'Malky, run!'

But McKeown was frozen to the spot, eyes wide.

Something clattered off the back of Shepherd's head and he sprawled forward. A kick to the side and he played dead.

'We need to go!' The voice, behind him, and so familiar.

The other guy, McKeown's attacker, was back on his feet. 'Grab them, let's get out of here.'

Shepherd looked up and saw Hunter and McKeown helped up to the back of the lorry.

'Sod this.' The big goon picked the other goon right off his feet and chucked him in the back. Poor guy was screaming.

Shepherd pushed up to standing and charged at the big one. This time he wasn't so lucky.

He caught a forearm in the throat and went down, feeling like his voice box was exploding.

The goon stood over him, pointing a gun at him. 'Bang, bang.' He tossed it in the air, caught the barrel and smashed the gun into Shepherd's temple.

He lay there and all he could do was listen to the lorry trundling away.

He didn't black out, but he felt like he should've.

Or did he?

Abducting Malky and Hunter. And Becky.

Shite. This was a complete disaster.

He tried to get up, but his legs wouldn't work.

'Luke?' The sun was blocked out. 'Are you okay?' A female voice.

He squinted and tried to see who it was.

Angela Caldwell, kneeling next to him.

He collapsed onto the pavement. 'They've got Malky. Hunter. Becky.'

She smiled at him. 'They've not got Becky.'

20

BAIN

This just gets worse.

'Shepherd's trouble.' I look at Bonzo, who's still got that balaclava on, not really paying attention. 'We should've taken him.'

The lorry rumbles as we drive, shaking everyone about. Christ knows where we're going. Hope it's getting away from that lot. Could do without speaking to my old colleagues.

'And we sure as hell should've taken *her*.'

Not many people bigger than both Hunter and Shepherd, but Bonzo is. He's *massive*. Like someone left a baby on a radioactive island in the Pacific and went back to find a giant. His sleeves are cut off at the shoulders, showing off flab, hair and thick muscle. Aye, you don't want him on your case. And he looks right at us now. 'Are you trying to tell me something, amigo?'

'I *told* you it was Becky. Your boss isn't going to—'

'Shut your mouth. She wasn't there.'

Shite. 'Really?'

But instead of smashing my face in, Bonzo grabs Hunter and hauls him to his feet, then starts strapping him against the wall. Unlike Hunter to put up no fight, but he's been through the mill, shall we say. And he's hanging there like Christ on the cross. Bonzo grabs his throat and squeezes. 'Now, son, you're going to talk.'

Christ, Hunter looks a broken man. A deep cut out of his cheek. Big bruises already forming around both eyes. All that time he gave the chat about how hard he is, all that martial arts bollocks and here he is, as weak as a day-old kitten. And as blind.

Bonzo points his gun at Hunter, pressing it into his eye socket. 'Two ways this goes, amigo.' He nudges the gun against his cheek. 'One, you talk to us, we let you go.' Then the gun goes against his forehead. 'Two, I shoot you. You die. Either way, you talk. It's whether you're walking away.'

'I'm telling you nothing.' Hunter spits blood in his face.

Bonzo sighs as he tears off the balaclava. Stares at it, then tosses it to the floor. His face is a criss-crossed mess of scar tissue. Bar fights and God knows what else. He holds on to the strap as we go around another bend. 'Thought it would go that way. Always the hard ones that think they're strong enough to endure this.' He presses the gun into his face again. 'So, one last chance. Live or die?'

'Piss off.'

'Suit yourself.' Bonzo straps a pair of brass knuckles around his meaty paw. 'Where is Becky?'

'No idea.'

Bonzo flexes his hands, then smacks Hunter in the gut.

He coughs like he has a fatal case of Covid. Tearing his lungs apart.

'Well, Craig, let's say I believe you. You've been a bit loose with your words.' Bonzo stares at the knucks. 'Who have you been investigating?'

Hunter hacks up a big lump of something. 'Piss off.'

I wave a hand between them. 'Mate, you'll kill him at this rate. Our friend won't be pleased.'

Bonzo sniffs.

I turn to Hunter. 'Craig. Mate. If you know…'

He's swaying, side to side like a dazed boxer. 'You're a coward, Bain. Nothing but a coward.'

'I'm the coward?' Makes us laugh. 'Craig, you're the one who attacked us in a phone box. Then denied you had the stones to attack us. How's that not cowardly?'

'Piss off.'

I point at the brass knuckles then beckon for Bonzo to hand them over.

He shrugs and tosses them.

I catch them and give them a good once over. Nice fit to them, have to say. 'Craig, you don't want me punching you with these on. Because once I start, I won't stop.'

'Piss off.'

'You've been working on the drugs squad. We want to know what you know.'

'I know sod all. Got kicked back to the MIT this morning.' Hunter spits on the floor. That wound on his cheek is leaking like a bastard. 'Sent me back to Cullen.'

Maybe he doesn't know anything more than what he spilled on that podcast.

Sod it, I slug him in the gut.

Crack.

Shite. Think I've broken something, but what's there to break in his gut?

He's gone all white, even with all that blood pouring down his cheek.

Brilliant.

Another punch, in his hip this time.

Another crack.

But he's being all stoic. Sucking in deep breaths.

'Craig, pal, just open up to me. Tell us. What have you got on him?'

'Him? Nothing. I've done nothing... but... look at CCTV footage... for six... months... That's it.'

Could well believe it. But I'm assuming it's bollocks, so I'll switch tack here. 'Where's Nina?'

'Who?'

'Nina Robertson.'

'No idea who that is.'

'The murder suspect, you fanny!'

'Like I said, I just got put on that case today. No idea who she is. Just...' He winces at something. Then shakes and shivers. 'Just doing door-to-door.'

The lorry turns a corner and speeds up. Hope we're on the A1 or the bypass. Miles away from Cullen and his gang.

'Where's Becky?'

Hunter just grins at us.

'The lassie you were taking back to the station. Where is she?'

Hunter winces. 'He's on to you.'

'Who is?'

'Shepherd.'

Can't help but laugh. 'That prick's useless.'

'Well, he knows that idiot over there is the Secret Rozzer.'

I look over and he's watching Malky McKeown.

Christ, Malky is a useless prick. Elvis wouldn't have made that mistake.

'Craig, where's Nina?'

He looks right at us, blood shrouding his eyes. 'Should ask Becky, shouldn't you? Oh, but you don't have her.'

Shite.

We're screwed here.

I toss the knucks back to Bonzo and sit on the bench next to Malky. 'What's going on, Malky?'

He shrugs. 'Shepherd can't know I'm the Secret Rozzer.'

'I mean, Shepherd knows you've been working with me. Two and two, pal.'

'Aye, but...' Malky swallows hard. 'I was careful. Ke— Our *friend* told me to be careful about it. Got some help with a pal of his. Charlie helped too. There's no way they could've traced it back to me.'

Charlie Kidd, though.

'Been on his payroll a while?'

He nods. Doesn't look at us.

'Threats against your bird?'

'Aye, Eva.' Now he looks at us. 'He got someone following Apinya?'

Apinya... Christ. I can't even think about it.

'Right. Showed me live video of someone outside the house. Her hanging out washing. I mean...' Christ, my hand is shaking.

'Malky, what did Cullen ever do to you?'

'Upset my wife. Treated her like shite.'

'When was this again?'

'That case with the missing schoolgirl. The disabled one.'

That case? I remember that. She was flirting with Cullen something rotten and for once he kept it in his pants.

Christ, talk about blowing it all out of proportions. But this isn't time to argue with him.

'Thing is, Bri, he's actually okay. Our friend. Don't mess with him and it's fine. And he pays well.'

Aye, and don't swan up demanding smoothies and answers.

I slump back on the bench. 'Our friend's not happy about losing his ex.'

'You don't think I know that?' Malky shakes his head. 'I tried to get her location out of Becky, but... She told me she doesn't know where Nina is.'

'Believe her?'

'No.'

'We were going to take her, Malky. What happened?'

'No idea. Put her in the car, then Craig talked to Shepherd, then I got in the car and she'd vanished. Just me and Hunter.'

I look around the back of the lorry. The thin light, the darkness at the back. 'Shite.'

'I'm not sure how much use she'd have been, Bri.'

'She talk to Hunter when you were driving?'

'A bit, maybe.'

Bastard. Stupid bastard.

Bonzo lumbers over to us. 'Good work, amigo.'

I peer up at him. 'What is?'

Bonzo claps Malky on the arm. 'You confirmed that Becky knows where Nina is.'

Malky gives him a "did I" look, but it soon becomes an "I did" look. 'Cheers.'

'Because of that, our friend got one of his people to hack into Nina's phone. We can't get her location, but there are a few texts to Becky. She's going to drop off the messages later.'

I look up at the boy. 'Told you we should've taken her.'

'Don't you see?' He thumps my arm and it's like being hit by a fridge. 'If you'd taken her, she would've said nothing. As it is, we can follow her.'

I give the boy the nod. 'Don't disagree, pal.' Then lean forward and lick my lips. 'Thing is, she's bound to be in the police station and we need to get her out.'

Another thump of meaty paw against my arm. 'Amigo, you two get to rescue her from a police station!'

21

CULLEN

Cullen leaned against the corridor wall and sucked in a mouthful of canteen coffee. Bitter and strong. He swallowed it. 'How is he?'

'Shepherd?' Angela looked up from her phone. 'He'll live.'

'Still, you were lucky you got him.'

'Aye, but you were lucky Shepherd managed to clue in Hunter. His quick thinking, told me to take Becky.'

'Aye, that's impressive work.' Cullen took another sip. 'No sign of them?'

'Elvis is checking for that lorry, but...' She grimaced. 'It's not looking good.'

'Figures.' Cullen nodded at her. 'Dump it somewhere, transfer to another vehicle.'

'Right. We'll look for that too.'

'How did Luke find out Malky McKeown is the Secret Rozzer?'

'Charlie Kidd.'

'Him.' Cullen squeezed the cup, almost pushing the coffee over the lip. 'He's involved?'

'I know.'

'Can't believe I trusted him. And Malky. Christ, I was supporting his application for DS.'

'Really? Were you actually supporting it or just telling Malky you were? Or was the idea to promote him away from your team?'

'Genuine support.' Cullen tipped the coffee into the middle bit and tossed the empty into the bin. 'Let's do this.' He entered the room and sat opposite Becky.

Angela joined him and set the machine going. 'For the record, present are myself DS Angela Caldwell, DI Scott Cullen and Rebecca Crawford, AKA Becky.' She looked across the table. 'You have been advised of your rights and cautioned regarding potential charges, you have acknowledged those rights in writing and have waived those rights so that you may speak with us of your own free will, without benefit of legal assistance.'

'That's right.'

'Okay, then, let's get started.' Angela leaned forward, arms folded. 'Where's Nina?'

'No idea.'

'Did she kill him?'

'Kill who?'

'Dale Mitchell.'

'Don't know who that is.'

'Did *you* kill him?'

'No!'

Angela reached into a folder and produced some photos. 'See, we've got a few stills taken from some video footage recorded last night. Shows you and Nina running away from her apartment.'

'Sure that's from last night?'

'Sure.'

Becky stared at the table, but not at the photos. 'Well, I don't remember it.'

'You told our officers you were in the bar all night.'
'Right.'
'But you weren't.'
'I...' She shut her eyes. 'Christ.'
'Becky, just tell us the truth. That's all we're asking here.'
She looked up at them. 'Look. He's bad news.'
'Dale?'
'Right.' Becky flared her nostrils. 'Like I told your guys. Always hitting on women in the Deb.'
'Was he hitting on Nina?'
She nodded. 'And she was loving it. Flirting back. Took him up to her flat.'
'So who killed him?'
'Not me!'
Cullen leaned forward, resting his elbows on the wood. 'Help me understand what really happened there, Becky, because I'm having trouble seeing the truth in this.'
'But I *am* tell—'
'No, Rebecca, you're not. And it ends now.'
'I'm telling you the truth.' She shut her eyes. 'There's nothing to tell, I wasn't there.'
'Becky, you've lied to the police in the past.'
She nibbled at a fingernail. 'I'm sorry about that.'
'Okay, but how about you explain these video stills?'
'I don't know anything.'
'You're going to prison for a very long time. Murder is one thing, but when it's by a woman, it'll be all over the papers. That'll be the legacy you leave. Anyone looking for your name will find stories of how you were a murderer. So. Who killed him? You or her?'
'Nobody. We found him in the bath.'
'But you didn't leave the bar.'
'Nina texted me.'
'Why?'

'Because he'd died!'

'What, in the bath?'

'Right. Must've had a heart attack.'

'Becky, someone hit him with a paperweight. Knocked him out. Then drowned him.'

She sucked in a deep breath.

'Was it you?'

She shook her head, but it was more like in disbelief than in denial.

'Becky, you need to come clean here.'

'There's nothing to tell. I wasn't there!'

Cullen stared at her, analysing a confused and lost woman. Someone who'd suffered her own ordeals over the years, who'd been exploited. But still, she was lying.

But why?

To protect herself?

Or to protect her friend?

Sod it.

Cullen stood up and grabbed the door handle. The power of a positive confrontation, using her formal name, telling a subordinate to take her into custody and being prepared to walk out of there. The next person to speak lost, and he had nothing to say. 'Sergeant, can you take Rebecca to processing and charge her?'

'On it.' Angela was on her feet too.

The Sergeant tilted his head to the door. 'Come on, Becky.'

But she stayed sitting, rooted to the spot. 'I didn't want Nina to shag him.'

And there it was.

Cullen settled back in the seat. He motioned for Angela to do the same.

Becky was chewing at her lips, but it was like she was chewing over how much of the truth to spill. 'I met him a few months ago.

Found each other on pogger. It's a hook-up app. Met him at my flat, shagged him, then he didn't call me back. And I kept seeing him in the bar, but I avoided him. Didn't see him for all of lockdown.'

'Until tonight?'

'Right.'

'Why did you kill him?'

'I couldn't handle Nina making the same mistake. So I went to warn her.'

Cullen sat there, waiting. 'About what?'

'He's a coke dealer. Load of bars around know about him. The Deb's the only one that turns a blind eye.' Becky tucked her hair behind her ears. 'And Nina found this bag of his, full of coke. A lot of coke. Two bricks of it. The only way he could get that is if he was working for her ex, and if he was working for her ex then he'd know where she lived and this was a set-up. So she was trapped. Backed into a corner. She lost it. Grabbed her paperweight from the table, went into the bathroom and... he was in the *bath*. Who does that? But she still... She... She hit him, then drowned him. I tried to stop her, but... She was too strong, kept pushing me away, kept on holding him under and... And he died.'

Cullen looked at her and finally got the sense she'd just told them the truth. If it had been a lie, a good lie, then she would've blamed it on some random guy. An intruder. No, something happened that no one expected and the cast of thousands dwindled to two, or one. 'Where is Nina?'

Becky just shook her head.

'What made her flip out about the coke?'

Becky shrugged. 'Thing is, Thornton wanted his coke back, but he didn't know that Nina took Dale out.'

'Thank you for your honesty. Rebecca. I appreciate it.' Cullen patted Angela on the arm. 'Take her downstairs. A few hours in a cell might soften her up. Right now, we've got enough to charge her with. A few months in prison will be a nice little treat.'

But all those tricks, those little threats, tried and trusted over years of use and refinement... They weren't working on Becky. She wasn't going to open up any more. She just got up and let Angela lead her out into the corridor.

What a life she'd led. A tragedy that kept on getting worse.

Cullen ended the recording. He still didn't know if she'd been the killer or not, but she'd go down trying to save her friend. From what?

That coke sent her rage spiralling. Why?

And they didn't have it in evidence. So Nina still had it.

Great.

Cullen sucked in a deep breath and stepped out into the corridor. He was hankering for another coffee.

Vicky Dodds was striding towards him, her eyebrows raised. She tugged at his sleeve and led him back into the interview room, then nudged the door behind them.

'What's up?'

'Long story, Scott. But I heard about Luke. Is he okay?'

'Big Luke'll be fine.'

Vicky looked around the room like the walls literally had ears. 'I need to tell you something.'

'Go on?'

'He's not who you think he is.'

'Vicky, I've worked with him for over ten years. He was my DS when I was an Acting DC in that team.'

'Right, and you think he's still a DS after all these years?'

'Aye.'

She shut her eyes, sighed, then reopened them again. 'Luke's working for Professional Standards and Ethics.'

'No, he's just back from his tenure there.'

'His tenure didn't end. He's a DCI. And he's investigating *you*.'

22

SHEPHERD

'Just hold still!' DS Holdsworth held Shepherd in place. Shepherd's head throbbed, but most of it was a mental pain. Anguish over losing his main suspect.

Malky McKeown.

What Eva had told him put him square in the frame. Their leaker. The Secret Rozzer.

Just why? What had Cullen ever done to him? Was it all about power and control? Had Cullen been involved with Eva?

Surely if he had, it would've been when he was seeing Sharon McNeill. And nothing got past her.

Holdsworth did something that made Shepherd's wound sting. 'There you go.'

Shepherd looked around at him. 'That's it?'

'That's it.' Holdsworth snapped the First Aid Kit shut, then stood up. 'I'm no doctor, but I have been trained in certain matters, shall we say.' He patted Shepherd's shoulder, right where it hurt the most. 'You're clear for duty, Luke.'

'Don't need to see the Duty Doctor?'

'Nothing concerns me about your condition.'

'Okay, cheers.' Took Shepherd three goes to stand up, by which time Holdsworth had left the room.

What a bloody mess.

Everyone would be talking about him, about how he'd lost two officers.

Actually, no. The truth was, he'd been tailing them. But so had whoever it was took them. A lorry on that side of the road. They'd known where they'd be.

And Christ, they were after Becky, weren't they? She should've been in the back of the car.

Losing McKeown, Hunter and Becky would've been a perfect mess.

Angela Caldwell may be many things, but Hunter's quick thinking got Becky out of there.

'Sarge?' Elvis was outside, looking like he was being told to enter the bear's den. 'Got a sec?'

Shepherd felt dizzy, like he was eight years old and had been spinning around like a daftie. He had to sit down again. 'What's up?'

'I've been working on this podcast lark.' Elvis scratched at his sidies. 'Thing is, everything points to Bain being involved, like she said.'

'Eva?'

'Right. But… I mean, I helped him with the technical stuff when we did *our* podcast, but that was it. We recorded together, I uploaded it. But the stuff Charlie Kidd's saying, it was all Malky.'

'So, why do you think Bain's involved?'

'Because he owns the Cheeky Judge. And he's been illicitly recording people in there. Hard to get that level of quality unless the whole bar's wired for sound. Mics around and beneath each table, great set-up but shoddy recordings, which means Bain can't prove anything. He's shite at recording, so what he heard he knows. Trouble is, with his credibility, he has no outlet for it directly and officially. Not to mention the recordings would be illegal.'

'I need evidence, though. Have you got a warrant?'

'I asked Cullen for it, Sarge, but haven't heard anything.'

'I'll chase it up.' Shepherd tried to stand again, but needed a bit longer. 'We should get someone around there to make sure Bain isn't in there dismantling everything.'

'Sure thing.' Elvis was scratching his sidies like he'd been bitten by a ton of midges. 'I feel like a bit of a dick for trusting him. I mean, I defended him to people. He's an angry man, but he can be kind and loyal. He helped my career a couple of times, but then I find out he's doing this shit?'

'What about his co-conspirators?'

'Well, I've never liked Malky, Sarge.'

'Why?'

'Just hate the guy. He's a total dickhead.'

Shepherd laughed. 'Fair enough.'

The room darkened and Cullen loomed in the doorway. 'Elvis, could you give us a minute?'

'Sure thing, sir.' Elvis gave a last look at Shepherd, then scuttled off out of there, leaving the door open behind him.

Shepherd sat back in his chair. 'You got that warrant?'

'Warrant?'

'For The Cheeky Judge.'

'Right. Aye, it's with Ally. He didn't want me approving it on my own.'

Which puzzled Shepherd. Then again, Davenport was the whole reason he was there. 'What's up?'

Cullen took the chair opposite. He looked at the door, frowned then looked back at Shepherd. Gave him the up and down. 'You're investigating me?'

Shite.

It had all been going so bloody well.

Shepherd had infiltrated his group and was digging, but finding nothing. Yet.

He was so close, but now it was going to be impossible.

Shepherd sat there, acting like a rock. 'Investigating you?'

'Cut the shit, Luke.' Cullen seemed to shiver. 'I *trusted* you.'

'What are you talking about?'

'Seriously, I'm not in the mood.' Cullen jabbed a finger. 'Why?'

Shepherd could deny it, pretend there was nothing going on. Or he could fess up. Or... 'Scott, I can't talk.'

Cullen lowered his head. 'So it's true?'

Shepherd looked up at the ceiling, looked over at the door. Anywhere but at Cullen. 'Who let slip?'

'Any time you share a secret, you make it more likely it'll leak.'

'Vicky Dodds?'

'It doesn't matter, Luke.' Shepherd finally looked at Cullen, but instead of rage, it was fear dancing in his eyes. 'Please, tell me the truth here. Am I in the shit?'

Shepherd had the upper hand. He outranked Cullen. So what if he'd found out about the investigation? Once Shepherd had collated all the evidence, there'd be a price to pay. 'I honestly don't know, Scott. This Secret Rozzer shit is going to stick to you.'

'It's all bollocks, Luke. They think I'm some apex shagger. I was *sexually abused* as a kid.' Cullen was crying. Tears sliding down his cheeks. 'You've no idea what I've been through. All those years of... of her mind games. Seeping into my head. I thought I'd overcome it, but I was... I was...' He rubbed at his eyes. 'Christ, I was just deluding myself. Replacing her toxic shit with my own toxic behaviour. I'm not proud of myself, but...'

Shepherd reached over and gripped his shoulder. 'It takes a

lot to recognise that, Scott. A lot more to change. And you have changed.'

'So why am I being investigated?'

'Because we've received a treasure trove of intel on you. Breaking drug investigations to get your man. Or woman. Covering over murder attempts by colleagues. Hell, you even falsified pension documentation for Angela Caldwell.'

'Shite.' Cullen stared up at the ceiling. 'That's…'

'I think that'll be the coup de grace, though. The finisher.'

Cullen shook his head. 'Luke, all the stuff they've been leaking about me, all of those actions. It was approved by Methven, by Cargill, by Turnbull. Even Soutar.'

'Then you'll be fine.'

'Aye, but it all went through Methven and he's off the board. Paralysed from the waist down and refusing to speak. Same with Soutar. Well, not the paralysis bit.' Another shake of his head that travelled down his body. 'Bain has it in for me. I don't know why. Maybe it's because I used to report to him, like I did to you. Then when I became his peer, then his boss…' He snorted. 'Thing is, he saved my life once. Like seven years ago. And I thought we were okay. Usual nonsense with him, where you could never tell if he was joking or whatever. And recently, there were so many times I chose to keep him on the force. Stood up for him to Methven. But he forced my hand, Luke. All the games he plays… And now… Now he's not a cop and he's got this massive inheritance, maybe he's using it to get back at me for some daft reason like I called him when his toast was in the machine and it burned. Who knows.'

'Scott, he owns the Cheeky Judge.'

'Jesus Christ.' Cullen smashed a fist off the table. 'He's been recording us in there. That's how it got to the Secret—' He stopped, frowning. 'Is he The Secret Rozzer?'

Shepherd shook his head. 'I've banned all serving cops

from going there. Watch the announcement come down tomorrow.'

'But the cat's out of the bag. Right? Who knows what else he's got on us.'

'Which is why I need that warrant.' Shepherd stared at him. 'Scott, I'll see what I can do to clear this. You're a good cop, if a bit of a cowboy.'

'Cheers, Luke, but I think I'm insulated here, you know? I have plenty of notes of my own. I mean, it might not be comfortable but I'll come through it.'

'It's going to be an uphill battle for you. Weeks of questioning. And I don't know what the end result will be.'

Cullen rubbed at his neck. 'If I go, I won't be going alone.'

'If I was you, I'd be shaking down my little black book.'

Cullen grinned. 'I have no idea what you mean.'

'It's—'

Someone knocked on the door. 'Luke?'

Sounded like Elvis.

Shepherd looked at Cullen. 'Are we good?'

'We're cool.' Cullen got up.

Shepherd tried to stand, but that wasn't happening. Holdsworth shouldn't have cleared him for duty. He shouted, 'Come in!'

Elvis barrelled in, lugging a laptop. 'Sarge, been thinking about what you just said, so I've run Bain's location.'

Cullen swivelled around, scowling. 'Elvis, you don't have a warrant for that.'

'I, eh, kind of do.' Elvis brushed at his sidies until the bristles stuck out like cactus spines. 'Long story, but it turns out there's a permanent surveillance request on his phone.'

Cullen looked over at Shepherd and mouthed, 'You?'

Shepherd gave the slightest nod, but kept his focus on Elvis. 'Go on?'

'Well, his phone's off right now, but Bain's been in central

Edinburgh.' Elvis swivelled the laptop around to show a map with several dots. 'Today.'

That partially tallied with Shepherd's knowledge. Thing is, Bain was in Dundee last night, before he was going to head back north. Way back north, to his home.

Lying sod.

Shepherd got out his phone and pulled up the web page. Took a few seconds to start working, but it found the car tracker he'd put on Bain's car when he was up at Bain's home two weeks ago. Still working and it zoomed in on the location. Now, Shepherd had to get to his feet. 'He's outside the station!'

23

BAIN

I should get out of the car, but something's stopping me. My own car.

Coward! Open the door and get out! St Leonard's station is right there! Becky Crawford is inside!

But I can't. Can't do anything, even with everything that's hanging over us. Keir Thornton and his goons, threatening Apinya and the wee one.

'Malky, this is too much.'

He looks at us like I've finally lost it. 'What are you talking about?'

'This.' I wave a hand in the direction of the station. 'Breaking into a police station to abduct some lassie. That's crossing a line.'

He laughs at us. 'Brian, you've pissed on that line so many times you don't even remember there even being a line.'

'That's a bit harsh.'

'Is it?' Malky laughs. 'You're the arch rule breaker.'

'Aye, but I used to do it for good and now... it's for Keir Thornton.' I let out a deep breath. 'I mean... How the hell did you get involved in this?'

'He came knocking one day. Threatened me. Like I said back in that lorry, Brian, he treats you well. Good bit of cash in hand. And he remembers. Whatever anyone does to us, we've got his word. He's broken a few legs for me.'

'You're serious?'

He nods.

Christ. Well, I'd mis-underestimated Malky. Is that the word? Either way, I thought he was a bit of a fanny. A useless sod like Elvis. But he's got teeth. And balls of steel.

'Come on, Bri. We get in there, grab her, get out and put her in the back. Even if they catch up with us, your motor goes like shit off a shovel.'

He's got a point. The Duchess Mark Two is a wild one. Untamed, beautiful and a hell of a beast—should see her sailing up the A9 past Inverness, like a space rocket.

I look over at him and maybe, just maybe, the prick's got a point. 'This is it for you, isn't it?'

He nods. 'One last job. He's setting me up in a place near Fort William. Still working for him, but a nice little nest egg and all that. New ID. New name. Me and Eva.' He looks down at his phone and his cheek twitches a wee bit.

'Aye, let's do it.' I open the door and hop out. Don't think about it, just act.

Malky's ahead of me, striding across the tarmac and holding the door for us. 'I'm leading in here, okay?'

'Sure thing, amigo.'

He winces at the use of Bonzo's favourite word, but goes inside and walks up to the door through to the back office, swiping his warrant card against the reader. It buzzes and he opens it.

'Malky?' Big Colin's head appears above the front desk. Massive it is too, and shaved, but not close enough to hide the severe ginger. Like he's tipped food colouring all over his bonce. 'Thought you were over with Drugs at Fettes?'

'Got sent back this morning. Working for the Happy Gang again.'

Colin laughs. 'Getting high on somebody else's supply, were you?'

'Something like that.' Malky thumbs at us. 'Mind Brian?'

'Who could forget.' Colin sips his tea. 'Thought they drummed you out.'

Christ, I'm sweating here. My balls are like a marsh. 'Aye, but the dozy twats forgot that I was lead on a case they hadn't solved. Some prick accidentally arrested a loonie in a park, so I've got to add my tuppence worth.' I give him a shrug, like "what can you do?". My oxters are an absolute midden.

'Sounds about right, aye.' Colin picks up his paper and sits back down. 'See you around, lads.'

Malky batters through the door and I almost bump into him. 'Close call, Bri.'

'Tell me about it.' Walking down these corridors as a civvy, and a wanted one at that, is seriously weird. Every door we pass has a memory. Berating someone in here, belittling someone in there, interviewing a load of bams and scrotes in there and there, oh and getting my arse handed to me in there.

What a life.

Malky turns the corner and stops dead. Fists clenched.

Ah shite, what now?

'Hey, Lauren, thought you were up in Fife?'

Here I am, bollocks deep in the station and we've been caught by one of Cullen's maidens. Christ!

'Malky, aye. We just got back with the victim's parents. Si's dropped them off down at the mortuary to identify their son.'

'Horrible, eh?'

'Tell me about it.' Still can't see her. 'What brings you here?'

'Cullen called me. Told us to take a tilt at Becky, maybe I can get anything out of her.'

Christ's sake, hurry up! I'm a sitting duck!

'Why you?'

'Interviewed her back in the day. Mind that case. Kenny Falconer?'

'Before my time.' Can see her now—she's frowning. Doesn't believe a word he's saying. 'Thing is, Scott asked *me* to interview her.'

'How about we do it together?'

She purses her lips, considering it.

'You've had a long drive, Sarge. Get a coffee and I'll catch you in the room.'

She's thinking about it, but tiredness overcomes her suspicion. 'Fine. I've booked room three.'

'Nice one.'

She brushes past him and frowns at us. 'Brian? What are you doing here?'

I stare at my shoes. 'Got to speak to Luke Shepherd. Some dick's been leaking information on a podcast. He thinks it's me!'

She looks at us like she knows it is. 'Well, good luck with that.' She walks off along the corridor.

And we both let out deep breaths.

'Malky. Go get Becky.'

He trudges through to the holding area. This is the bit that's got me sweating buckets, I tell you. Navigating her out of a cell, signing forms. Christ, you can see why this is Malky's last job, eh?

But we're in luck! Becky's standing there, head bowed. She looks up and her eyes go wide.

Martin's standing next to her, his belly puffing out his shirt. 'Boys, what's up?'

Malky grins at him. 'Got to escort her to another interview.'

'What?' Becky's frowning. 'Why?'

'Sorry, but this is the price of lying to the cops.' Malky grabs her arm and hauls her through. 'Cheers, Martin!'

The security chief just nods. Couldn't care less.

I duck my head and follow them, trying to avoid any prick seeing us.

Why the hell did I have to come inside? Aye, because Malky is a lying shite. Thornton doesn't trust him. I certainly don't. And Becky doesn't. 'Where are you taking me?'

'To see a pal.' Malky swipes the door and we're back in the entrance foyer.

Colin's stuck in his paper, not even paying attention.

Fifteen steps to the door. Out into the cold morning. Then another thirty to my car. I plip the lock after ten. Closing in on it, me and Malky and Becky.

A hand on my collar.

I shake it off and spin around.

Luke Shepherd's towering over us. 'You're coming with me.'

'Am I hell!' I step forward and stick the nut on him. He's a foot taller than me, so I miss his nose and only get his jaw. But he goes down, tumbling against a motor, sprawling over it.

'Get in.' I open the back door and shove Becky in, then get behind the wheel. Don't even wait for Malky to shut his door before gunning it and shooting across the car park.

Onto St Leonards Street and heading to the swimming baths, and get a green at the lights, turn left to go through the park.

Free and clear.

I swivel the mirror around to look at Becky. 'You're going to tell us where Nina is.'

'I don't know.'

'You do, so don't start with your nonsense. We know you've been texting her. Now, you tell us where she is and we let you go. Otherwise, we drop you with her ex. And he's not your biggest fan. And he'll get the information out of you by slightly uncivil means. So, you can trust us, or you can trust us to drop you deep in a well you won't be able to crawl out of.'

Becky's looking out of the window. A friend's life or your own?

Not exactly a hard choice, is it?

She looks back at us. 'Okay.'

24

CULLEN

Cullen shot through the office and tore open Davenport's door. 'Sir!'

He looked up from his computer, scowling. 'What?'

Cullen was panting hard. Too much working, not enough working out. 'Bain's in the station.'

'Bain?' Davenport shot to his feet. 'Why?'

'Don't know.' Cullen turned around and raced back the way he came. He fished out his phone and called Elvis. 'You getting anywhere with the CCTV?'

'On it.'

Cullen held his phone out as Davenport caught up with him. 'Did you know I'm being investigated by Shepherd?'

Davenport shouldered through the door then clattered down the steps two at a time. 'You're asking me that *now*?'

'I know it's the truth, sir. He's undercover, investigating me.'

'Scott, there are bent cops here. Have been for years.' Davenport slowed as they walked along the downstairs corridor. 'Someone was on Dean Vardy's payroll, leaking shit to him.

How he was always one step ahead of us. Now someone's leaking shit on that podcast.'

'It's Malky McKeown.'

'What?'

'He's with Bain. When Hunter leaked on the podcast about the raid on the Deb, Malky must've told Thornton, who needed Dale to retrieve the coke. But Dale was dead. And they've taken Becky Crawford from custody.'

Davenport stopped dead. He swallowed hard and ran his hand across his forehead. 'Her? Why's she here?'

'You don't listen to my messages or read my texts, do you?'

'Jesus wept.' Davenport stormed off towards the front of the station. 'Becky Crawford is responsible for that case falling apart ten years ago. I've got sympathy for her plight, but her actions cost lives when Kenny Falconer escaped. That let Dean Vardy in. Now it's Keir Thornton's turn to make people's lives a misery.' He pushed through to the reception, where Big Colin was chatting to the cleaner. 'Where is he?'

Colin looked over. 'Where's who?'

'Never mind.' The door rattled as Davenport stormed outside.

Cullen put his phone to his ear. 'Getting anywhere?'

'Sorry, Scott.' Elvis sighed. 'System's buggered.'

'Right, right.' Cullen joined Davenport outside.

'Scott!' Shepherd was on his hands and knees, his mouth a bloody mess. 'Ally!'

Cullen sprinted over and helped him up, leaning him against a car. 'You okay?'

'Why does this keep happening to me?'

'Have you found Bain?'

'No, he did this to me!' Shepherd touched a finger against his lips. 'Christ, it's bloody agony.'

'Scott?' A tiny voice came out of Cullen's phone.

He put it to his ear. 'What's up?'

'I've got Bain's Tesla X driving off from the station, heading south.'

'Follow me!' Cullen raced over to his car and got in. His Golf might be a GTI, but that was no match for Bain's Tesla.

Still, he had to try.

He shot off across the car park and bombed into traffic, right in front of a bus. He floored it and overtook another one, sliding around it and back in. 'You got an update?'

'Aye, he's gone through the park.'

Cullen grunted, involuntary but it came out anyway, and shot through the red light and took the road into Holyrood Park. He closed on the roundabout. Left led back to the city, right on to Duddingston, Niddrie and Portobello. 'Elvis, which way?'

'Cameras in Duddingston and down in Holyrood, and he's not hit either of them.'

So he was still in the park.

Cullen had hope.

He hit the pedal and took the left, then again at the next roundabout, shooting through the park. No sign of Bain's car.

Wait. Up ahead, maybe a mile further on, passing through the next roundabout. Then the right past St Margaret's Loch.

Bain was climbing up Arthur's Seat.

Christ. That meant going back *there*...

Last time Cullen had been up this way, well... That was another story, but it was what was going to get him deep in the shit right now, if Shepherd had anything to do with it.

The things he'd done, covering up stuff. Just...

And Bain knew. He knew Cullen would follow. So he was playing him. Goading him.

As he climbed, the city's sprawl became visible through the grass and trees, then gone, hidden again. He passed the other loch, weaving around the tourists stopping to take photos, then into the car park behind the thin row of trees.

There.

A Tesla X parked on the left, its boxy weirdness sticking out like a sore thumb.

Cullen pulled in, grabbed his baton and got out.

Bain was standing by the car, talking on his phone. 'Sure about that, aye? Well, you're the boss.'

He was going to pay for all of this shite. It all started with him. It was going to end with him.

Becky was in the back, eyes wide, mouth hanging open. She'd spotted Cullen.

Down below, the university's two sites were separated by houses Cullen could never afford. The wind kicked up the perfume of early-flowering plants.

Up here, where he had watched a good friend lose his mind. Lose his job. Lose his life. Over four years ago, but it felt like yesterday.

He set off towards the car, gripping his baton tight.

Bain pivoted around and locked eyes with him. 'Ah, shite.'

Cullen reached his baton back behind his head, ready to swing.

Something cracked off the back of his knee and fire burnt up his leg. He rolled forward. Dropped the baton. It rattled over the tarmac. He tried to rock to the side, but someone stomped on his wrists, pinning him in place. The fire spread up his arms now.

Malky McKeown stood over him, grinning. 'Well, well, well.'

25

SHEPHERD

Shepherd was in the passenger seat, dabbing at his teeth with a paper tissue. Like fighting a nuclear bomb with a stick. He'd need dental work, but Christ knew when that would be. Have to go private, again.

Vicky took her eyes off the road long enough to look around at him. 'You okay, Luke?'

'Pretty far from okay.' Shepherd swayed as the car rounded the bend and he put his phone to his ear. 'Elvis? You got anything?'

'Well, no sign of Cullen's car, but...'

Vicky took the bend past the loch, about halfway along the road twisting around Arthur's Seat.

'It should be there.'

Cullen's Golf was trundling away, the door hanging open, driving off the edge towards the cliffs.

Shepherd pointed at it. 'There!'

Vicky screeched to a halt.

Shepherd had the door open before she stopped and raced across the tarmac. He hopped the barrier onto the grass.

But Cullen's car was nearing the edge of the cliff.

Shepherd raced to keep up with it, but it was getting faster and faster.

He couldn't see if anyone was inside.

And then it was gone, falling and tumbling down the hillside.

Shepherd had to catch a tree branch to stop following it.

Cullen...

Jesus Christ.

'Luke?' Vicky was behind him, taking it slower and more carefully. 'What happened?'

'Scott... His car.' Shepherd swallowed hard. 'It's...'

He'd been investigating Cullen. A good cop, or so they said. Maybe he was in deep, but maybe not.

She was frowning. 'Did he kill himself?'

All Shepherd had was a shrug. He tried to inch closer to the edge, but the wind was whipping around them.

A car door slammed behind them.

'Jesus.' Sharon joined them, hugging herself tight. 'This is where Bill Lamb died.'

'My God.' Vicky was crying. Such a strong woman, stern even, but she was reduced to tears now. Broken. 'All that shite. The podcast. Do you think he killed himself?'

Shepherd didn't know.

But Vicky was asking the question of Sharon.

'It's plausible, but...' She was crying too. 'Christ, Scott. You stupid prick.'

Vicky looked around at Shepherd. 'Come on, he wouldn't. If he was in that car, someone put him there.'

Shepherd stared at the ground, at the tyre tracks leading from the car park to Cullen's doom. 'Was he in it?'

'I don't know. Did you see him?'

'I can't say he wasn't, but why would he kill himself?'

Cullen was a tough son of a bitch.

Chasing after Bain and Malky McKeown.

Maybe he was ambushed, maybe they killed him.

'Thing is, I can see it all play out in Cullen's head. Being up here, the site of Lamb's last moments. His friend. And you're right—that bloody podcast unearthing his past trauma, sharing it with the world. Made him follow a doomed cop who chose that way out. Lamb left a wife and two boys behind rather than facing the music for his crimes.'

'Aye, Cullen could easily have gone down that route.'

He looked at Sharon, then at Vicky. 'I'll call Yvonne.'

Vicky nodded, but hugged Sharon and it was like she was trying to move her away from the edge, either to stop Sharon joining her ex down there or to just stop her from looking.

Shepherd got out his phone and saw that he was still on a call with Elvis. 'Sorry, Elvis, I've got to—'

'There you are! I think I've got Bain's car leaving the park ten minutes ago.'

Shepherd stood there, trapped by indecision.

Go after Bain, or find out what happened to Cullen?

He needed to go for it.

He ran over to the pool car and got in.

26

BAIN

Malky pulls up at an address in Niddrie. Of all the places we could go, it had to be here. When I started in this infernal city, this place was all gunshots in the panes of glass and feral kids. Now it's starter homes and supermarkets.

Looks like nobody's in, but that's how she should be playing it. Half of Edinburgh's out looking for her, but Nina Robertson should be keeping the lowest of low profiles.

I look around at Becky in the back seat. 'You better pray she's still here, doll. Because if she's not, I'd rather not be wearing your Jimmy Choos.'

She's not looking at us. Some people, eh?

I get out into the stiff breeze. Look over at Arthur's Seat and see some flashing blue lights up there. I did what I had to, didn't I? Nothing can come between me and my family. Nobody can threaten us.

This is it. Get Nina, hand her over to the boss man and get the hell out of Dodge. Drive home, bunker down in the Highlands. Pay those boys from Glasgow to scope out the place for us, in case Thornton sends anyone my way.

Aye, like that'd work.

Only way out of this is to keep in with the big man. Do his dirty work for him. Keep him onside, give him no reason to come north. And just stay up there.

I'd got away from it all. But had to just twist the knife that little bit more, didn't I?

Bloody idiot.

Malky joins us. 'How you doing?'

'I'm done, Malky.'

One thing to ruin the life of a toe rag like Cullen, quite another to be threatening lassies. Young lassies too. Handing them over to animals like my new best mate Bonzo and his boss. And Christ knows what they'll do to them. Torturing's probably the least of it.

'Nina's going to die, isn't she? I can't...'

'After what we just did on that hillside?'

'That's different. Cullen had it coming to him.'

'Brian, you might think you can get out, but he'll kill Apinya.'

'I can't... But...'

He's right. I need to stay the course here. Gain influence with the big man. Only way to keep us safe.

'Used to be a hard lad, didn't you?' Malky stuffs his hands in his pockets. 'Talk the talk? But you can't walk the walk.'

'Malky, I...'

'Brian, you just have to do a few steps with me. This is our wives against some daft lassie. No contest.'

'I can't.'

'Sod it, then. Stay here.' He points at the Duchess. 'Stay with Becky. Make sure she doesn't go anywhere.'

I still don't know about this. Nobody knows the things I've done today, do they? But this... He's right. It's crossing a line.

Stop being a coward. Once I'm over it, I'll be Keir's boy. I've got umpteen years service as a cop. I know what I'm doing. Aye, it'd be a decent life. Don't need the money, but a boy like Keir having my back? Priceless.

And who am I kidding? Bursting a lassie out of the nick, doing what we did up on Arthur's Seat...

I stomp up to the door and peek inside. Tiny wee place on a long street. Nobody obviously watching us, but time is of the essence. Probably loads of people hiding out themselves.

Wee gate at the side, mind. Aye, that's the trick.

I turn back to Malky. 'I'm going in the back. Stay here and grab her.'

'Right-o.'

I hop over the gate and walk through to the garden, scraping a handful of harling off the side wall.

The garden's filled with more kids' shite than ours is, and it's about a tenth the size. Few big trees lining the place, so the pricks over yonder won't see me doing this.

Bunch my sleeve over my hand and think about punching it. But I try the door instead. And it opens, doesn't it? Stupid. Really stupid. Then again, if some big scary bastard comes to the front door, you want a quick exit. No messing with keys and handles and that.

I slide it open, super carefully, then slip inside.

Music's playing. The radio, I think. That Calvin Harris boy. Heard someone say he was worth three hundred million. Wee boy from Dumfries. Good on you, son!

FOCUS.

Christ.

Smells of fresh toast. Butter still out on the counter, big slab of it with a chunk taken out. No plate, no knife, and the toaster's still warm.

She's here.

Right.

I lock the door and take the keys, then set off through the bijou kitchen into a hallway.

Stairs up, same beige carpet as elsewhere. No photos on the walls, up or down. A strangely impersonal place, as I would've written in my notebook and read out in court.

A downstairs kludgie, but the door's open and the fan's off.

Front door, shoes and coat hanging up.

Leaving just one door down here. And a smell of toast.

Crunching.

Chewing.

Some shite on the telly playing too.

Bingo, there she is.

Nina Robertson. No' a bad-looking lassie, at all. But that's by the by.

'Here, Missy, it's—'

She swivels and hurls the plate at us. Bounces off my chin and I go down like a sack of unwashed tatties.

She jumps over us. I try to grab her but she's too fast.

Push up, get going. Wake up!

She's in the kitchen, at the door. Shaking the handle.

I reach into my pocket and dangle the keys. 'Looking for these?'

'Who are you?'

'Friend of your ex-husband's.'

She shuts her eyes. 'What's it worth?'

'What, to let you go?'

She nods. 'I'll do whatever you want. Whatever it is. Whatever you want. Please, just let me go.'

'Darling, you shouldn't make promises like that. I might want to amputate your leg and shag you from the side while you play the harmonica. Sad thing is, Nina,' she flinches at the mention of her name, 'neither of us has any power here. All the leverage is with your old man.' I step forward and grab her arm.

Tight enough that she won't bolt, which is so tight it makes her gasp.

'Let go of me!'

'Come on.'

She's struggling but you don't put in almost thirty years' service without being able to handle a daft wee lassie.

'Out we go.' I take her into the hall.

'I need my shoes.'

I laugh at her. 'I very much doubt that.' Wee bit of bother opening the front door one handed, but we're outside. Into the wind and rain.

And Keir Thornton's standing there, hands in pockets, grinning wide. 'Ah, Nina. Nice to see you again.'

27

CULLEN

Cullen felt like he'd died.
His skull was more lump than skin. Like someone had battered him with a golf club.
Oh, that's because they had.
Malky McKeown. And his swing was perfect.
A low rumble ran through him. Meant movement.
Sickly smell of passionfruit, but an artificial equivalent. And the dusty smell and taste of soot. From a diesel engine, one that hadn't been serviced in a while.
He blinked hard a few times and tried to adjust to the low light. Almost pitch black. Looked like a lorry, maybe. He was lying on his back, facing up. Three other shapes in here that could be people.
And he recognised two of them.
Bain, sitting cross-legged and humming a tune.
Someone with his head in his hands, with the outline of Malky McKeown.
The third guy was bigger than Hunter and Shepherd put together. His eyes adjusted to the light a bit and he saw a welt of scar tissue and rage.

Cullen tried to move but he was tied down.

'Easy there, amigo.' He didn't recognise the voice. Scottish, but hard to pin it down. Not Edinburgh, certainly. He braced against a bump, tugging at a handhold. 'Nice to see you back in the land of the living, sunshine.'

'Told you, it's Sundance.'

'Right.' The shape got up and moved over behind Cullen. Cullen felt the cold metal of a gun barrel against his neck, right over his brain stem. 'Where are you taking me?'

'To see a friend. Don't worry, you won't be alive much longer.'

Bain laughed. 'You tell him, Bonzo!'

Cullen thought he saw the whites of Bain's eyes looking at him. 'I'll make you pay for this.'

'Aye? You take contactless?' He howled with laughter.

McKeown wasn't joining in. Was he another prisoner? Or was he a reluctant accomplice?

Hard to tell.

The lorry shuddered to a halt and Cullen slid forward, the ties braking his momentum. 'Where are we?'

'Oh, you'll see.' The metal stopped kissing his neck and Bonzo thumped over to the back. He hauled open the gate and bright light bleached everything.

Made Cullen's head ache, his eyes sting.

Bonzo hopped down. Squelched like he'd landed on thick mud. Smelled like it too. But the dry tang of crops—wheat and barley. 'Bring him, amigo.'

Bain was eager to comply, coming over to untie Cullen's bonds. 'Oh, Sundance, what have you got yourself into?' Another laugh.

'Let me go.'

'No chance.' Bain tried lifting Cullen, but he was playing dead. 'Christ's sake, Malky, come here.'

'Right.' McKeown raised himself up and walked over. He set

about the ties and freed Cullen, then slapped on some handcuffs. 'Come on, then.'

As he was dragged by the pair, Cullen had just one word for McKeown. 'Why?'

'Why what?'

'Why have you done this to me?'

'Because you're a prick. Because you pissed off Eva. Because... Because you deserve it. Because your luck had to run out eventually, you pretty boy wanker. A guy like you gets made DS before me? Piss off! And a *DI*? I hate everything about you, your whinging, your insecurity, the way you confuse dumb luck with any actual skill. You deserved to be taken down a few pegs and embarrassed. I have underwear with more time policing than you do. And a DI going to recommend me for a promotion I deserved long before you could even spell sergeant. Piss off, Sundance.' He spat in his face.

All this for some trivial bullshit. Jealousy. Ego. Arrogance.

Christ.

The harsh daylight made him shut his eyes.

They eased him down so his legs were resting on the edge, then two splats as they jumped down.

Cullen could run for it, but he was handcuffed to McKeown and he was just broken. No energy in the tank. He looked at Bain. 'Brian, let me go.'

'Fat chance of that, dickhead.' He tugged at Cullen's sleeve. 'Let's get going.'

Cullen looked around. They were up high somewhere. Probably the Lammermuirs. Surrounded by wooden pallets, piled twenty metres tall. Enough to block out the morning sun. A thin lane led back the way, covered in damp mud and sliced open by tyre tracks. Another lane led on, and gave a view of a triangular mountain.

Traprain Law.

Cullen knew exactly where he was—five miles east of

Haddington, twenty-odd from Edinburgh. Not too far away, but close to the middle of nowhere.

McKeown waved over at Bain. 'Get the other one.'

'You do it!'

McKeown raised his cuffed wrist. 'Bit tied up at the minute.'

'Christ's sake.' Bain hopped up into the lorry.

Cullen needed to buy some time, to recover, to plan, then to escape. 'Malky, I was supporting your Sergeant's exams.'

'Aye.'

'That's it? Aye?'

'Sorry.'

Bain hopped down again. 'Mud's getting everywhere.' He reached in and grabbed a leg. 'Need a hand with this one and no sign of Bonzo.'

McKeown wandered over and grabbed another boot, then they tugged in unison.

Hunter sat on the edge of the truck bed, head swaying. His face was red and black, bruised and bloodied.

Cullen gasped. 'Craig!'

Hunter's right eye was swollen up, but his left focused on Cullen. 'Scott?'

Cullen tried to move forward. 'We're getting out of this, okay?'

'Don't kid yourself.' Bain hauled Hunter down and snapped on a pair of cuffs. He led him through the gap towards the hill.

A revving engine powered behind them and Bain yelped, pressing himself flat against the lorry.

A purple Tesla squealed to a halt and the door swung up like a seagull's wing. Keir Thornton stepped out and gave a round of applause. 'Lovely machine, Brian. Got to compliment you on that.'

Bain grinned. 'Want that washed and dried, mind.'

Thornton raised his thin eyebrows at him. 'O-kay.' He was massive, all thick muscle and straining sinew. The kind of physique you only got from illicit means—steroids, or newer drugs that were untraceable. He nodded his thick skull at someone. 'Bonzo, mind getting them out?'

'Boss.' The even bigger goon opened the back door and pointed his gun inside. 'No funny business.'

Nina was first out, bare feet splashing on the mud.

Then Becky, her tennis shoes caked in mud in seconds.

'Take them through.' Thornton watched Bonzo lead the women through the gap.

Cullen didn't know where they were going, but he could guess at what he was planning on doing to them. Part of the why still eluded him.

Thornton walked over and got in Cullen's face. 'Well, well, we meet again.'

'Let me go.'

Thornton looked him up and down, then at Bain and McKeown. 'That's not going to happen.' He looked at Bain. 'Well, I'd like to thank you for your help here. Didn't think you'd pull through, but you've done admirably.'

'No bother.' Bain sniffed, looking at Cullen. Then he punched him in the guts.

Cullen coughed hard. 'Let us go.'

Thornton laughed. 'Nope.'

'You'll have half of Police Scotland here before you know it. I'm telling you, let us go.'

Thornton laughed, hard. 'You stupid arsehole. You think you can dictate terms to me?' He licked his lips. 'I'm a kind man, Scott, so I'm giving you a choice. You can work for me, and I'll put you on my payroll. Malky here will tell you I'm very generous.'

Now it made sense.

Why Malky McKeown had done it. It wasn't because of some stupid history with Eva, something that barely happened. No, Malky McKeown was bent. Corrupt. And greedy.

'Malky, you're just a scumbag, aren't you?'

McKeown jerked forward, but Thornton stopped him.

'I have a place in my life for many scumbags, Scott.' Thornton got out a high-end smartphone and held it out to Cullen.

The screen was split in half.

The left showed a flat near Easter Road—where Hunter lived with Chantal Jain.

The right was from a car parked outside Livingston nick, watching Yvonne leaving the station, then following her down the road.

Cullen's stomach burned. Ice flowed down his legs, up his arms. 'No.'

'No?' Thornton put the phone away. 'So you're deciding that Yvonne dies in about ten minutes? Nice wee car crash on the M8. Shame if there's anyone else injured. That arsehole Terry Lennox is in the car with her. His death will be on your head, Scott. Both their deaths.'

Cullen had to fight against his instincts. This was how they'd got to McKeown. Leverage the partners. Standard tactic. 'No.'

'Okay.' Thornton looked away and shrugged. 'In that case, you're getting buried here. Got a load of hungry pigs who have a taste for pig meat. You won't be the first serving officer to go through them, believe me.'

Cullen was going to die. Same with Craig. They were no use to anyone dead. He looked Thornton in the eye. 'Fine.'

Thornton frowned at him. 'Fine?'

'I'll do it. Both of us will. Me and Craig. Stick us on your payroll. Whatever you want, we'll do it. Just don't harm Chantal or Yvonne.'

Thornton grinned wide. 'How can I trust you?'

'It's not about trust, it's about you having leverage over us. You've just shown me you've got men following them. I hate you and want you to die, but as long as you've got the woman I love in your sights, I'm your man.'

'I'm glad we have an understanding.' Thornton reached into his pocket, but this time he pulled out a gun. He pressed it against Cullen's chest, right over his heart. 'Malky, son, get that tarp out, would you?'

McKeown held up his cuffs. 'I'm a bit tied up.'

'It's just inside the bloody lorry.' Thornton shook his head, but watched as McKeown unfolded the tarpaulin one-handed.

Cullen stood there, blood pumping in his temples.

This was it.

He'd survived a golf club to the head just to be shot on a farm. Nobody would find his body. He'd just be a statistic.

And Malky McKeown. Leaking all that shite about him. Personal stuff. The *most* personal. His abuse as a child. At the hands of a teacher.

No, he wasn't getting away with it.'

Cullen tilted his head to the side. 'What are you going to do with Malky?'

Thornton frowned. 'What do you mean by that?'

'Well, he's compromised. People are on to him. A few warrants. His phone's tapped. You name it. He's no use to you now.'

'That's a good point, actually.'

'Let me take him in. Arrest him, charge him. You've still got leverage over him, so he'll keep quiet. It'll make me look good and I can be extremely helpful to you.'

Thornton narrowed his eyes, nodding slowly. 'Nah, sod that.' He shifted the gun from Cullen and shot McKeown in the head.

28

BAIN

Malky...

Jesus Christ.

He's a corpse now. Dead eyes staring up at the thunderclouds.

What the hell?

Why kill him? Why not Cullen? Or Hunter? Why him?

Thornton's crouching, undoing the handcuffs from Malky's wrist. Cullen's free now. And on his payroll.

Jesus Christ.

How did this end up so wrong?

Thornton tosses the gun onto Malky's corpse. I can see Cullen wanting to go for it, but he's smarter than the average bear. Just about. Thornton does a wolf whistle so loud only a football manager or a brickie could compete.

Two big lumps come out of nowhere and know precisely what to do. Grab each end of the tarp and drag Malky's body away.

He's pig meat now.

Jesus Christ.

'Come on, then.' Thornton unlocks Cullen's handcuff, claps him on the arm and leads him away.

Am I supposed to drag Hunter after them?

Should've thought this all through. Not that I had a chance. Or a choice.

Thornton's talking to Cullen like they're best buddies. Christ, I need to put a stop to this.

'Come on, big man.' I grab Hunter's arm and tug it, but he's not shifting, is he?

He looks down at me. 'I'm going to kill you.'

'Not the first person to say that, Craig. Now, come on.' I grab his arm again and he complies this time.

Finally.

Thornton's leading us down to a big barn. What's going on in there, I don't want to know. Doubt it's brewing hoppy craft beers.

Inside, the lights flicker on. Taking their time, mind. Place is massive.

That Becky lassie is sitting on a stool, head bowed.

Bonzo's guarding her and he's holding a Dirty Harry Magnum to her neck.

Thornton pushes Nina over to me. Lassie looks terrified.

Not surprised. Face to face with her ex-husband. And he's got guns everywhere.

'Thanks for helping me find her, Brian. You're worth your weight in brass.'

I laugh, way louder than I should. Got to keep in with the big boss, eh? 'Prefer to weigh myself in copper.'

He smiles at that, then goes head to head with his ex. 'Know what she's been doing?'

I give him a wee nod. 'Heard she killed some boy.'

'Right. Do you know who that boy is?'

'Nope.'

'Name's Dale Mitchell.'

'Still not ringing any bells, chief.'

'Right, well. I know him. And Nina knows I know him.' Thornton caresses her throat with his finger. 'See, as we drove here, I spent a bit of time with her, asking questions. I know when Nina's lying.' He grins. 'It's when she moves her lips.'

Nina is looking at us, pleading with those big doe eyes of hers.

I mean, talk about looking to the wrong saviour.

Thornton wraps a big bear arm around her. 'See, Nina had seen young Dale in the bar she worked in. The Debonair. Used to belong to Dean Vardy, but it got sold off to a legitimate businessman after he met his unfortunate end. Now, it turns out that Dale was dealing drugs to people in there. Students, drinkers, anyone who wanted a wee toot of coke. And he was working for my people.'

Nina shuts her eyes. 'Please, Keir. Let me go.'

'Last night, young Dale just so happened to be strolling along outside and spotted a bottle of red wine at a table. He couldn't help himself. Thing is, it wasn't put there by chance. No, Nina and Becky trapped him.'

'Keir, please.'

'He was a flirt. His big flaw. Seemed to prefer Nina over Becky. And she offered to take him upstairs.' Thornton snaps on a leather glove, a fancy black job. All shiny. 'Now, I don't know who killed him. Don't really care. He was in the bath, defenceless. One of them smacked him with a paperweight. Then held him under. Maybe it was Becky, maybe Nina. Maybe both. They're not saying.'

Nina shuts her eyes. Pish trickles down her legs. Poor lassie. Still, you suck the devil's cock and what do you expect?

Thornton pulls on the other glove. Doesn't seem to notice her accident. 'And you know, I don't really care if someone bumps off one of my low-level guys like Dale. Problem is, Dale had just got a re-up. A hundred grand's worth of coke. My coke.

A little birdie,' he side-eyes Malky's body, 'told me about a warrant so I needed someone to get it out of there. Dale got it before the cops turned up. But you grabbed hold of it. *My drugs, Nina. Mine.*'

I snort. 'That's shocking, so it is.'

'Isn't it?' Thornton walks over to a locker and takes out a big rifle. Sniper thing. Looks the business. And scary as. 'What's worse is Nina tried to blackmail me in return for my son.' He reaches over and unlocks my handcuff, separating me from Hunter. 'Drugs in exchange for my son. It puts a price on his head, too. A hundred grand. Makes you sick, doesn't it? But still, Nina's got the drugs somewhere. And she won't tell me where.' He cracks the rifle. Like in a film. God knows what it does, but it sounds mental. Makes her flinch, like. 'And she's *never* seeing her son again.'

Nina looks up at him. 'Keir, please. Let me—'

Thornton puts a finger to her lips. 'No, no, no. It's only a hundred grand.' He smiles at Bonzo. 'Hold her, would you?'

Bonzo gets hold of Nina from behind. She's freaking out. 'Keir, please. No!'

Thornton grabs me from behind now, like he's teaching me how to bowl, and uses my hands to grab the rifle. 'Nina, you should've stayed away. Kept to yourself. Called the cops, even.' He pushes my finger through the guard, resting it against the trigger. 'But you made it personal. He's *my* son.' Aims the sights at her head. Like playing a video game. 'Not yours. *Mine.*'

'Keir, please!' Tears are streaming down her cheeks. 'Don't—'

Thornton squeezes my finger and shoots her. Blood sprays the walls and she falls back.

The sound is deafening.

I want to drop the gun but he's holding it tight.

She flops back onto another tarpaulin, and I can't look at her.

Thornton whispers in my ear, 'Thank you, my sweet prince.'

I am absolutely buggered now. Good and proper. Being a bit bent is one thing, but now...

Thornton owns me.

I am going down with the Titanic here.

'Now, Brian.' Thornton lets go of the gun, but I don't. Daren't, even though my hands are shaking like the old boy's were before he popped his clogs. 'These two are witnesses, so I need you to kill them.'

Cullen and Hunter. Both looking shit scared. Cullen's got that stern look on his face, all determined, but Hunter can't bring himself to look at us.

I can't kill them.

I can still deny it was me who shot her. It wasn't me pulling the trigger, he was using me.

Thing is, that won't wash. Two cops as witnesses, but how long are they both staying alive?

I'm in the shite here.

And I've nothing to lose.

'Damn right I will!' I step forward and press the rifle into Cullen's face, right into his eye socket. Looks like he's been absolutely battered. Well, it's about to get a whole lot worse. 'Sundance, I'm going to savour this.'

'Stupid bastard, it's got your prints all over it. Neither you nor the gun will ever be found.'

'I don't care. I'm the guy who's taking you down.'

'What have I ever done that's so wrong?'

'My boy's in prison because of you!'

'He's there because he made a mistake that cost two people their lives. He deserves everything he gets.'

'I saved your life! All those years ago!' I press the gun deeper into his eye socket. Who cares what kind of mess it's going to make. 'You owe me for that!'

He's calm, though. 'This is your own fault, Brian. I've saved your career so many times over the last three years. Cleared shit with Methven, but you kept on screwing up. Flying to America without approval? No wonder you got kicked off the force. Now you own the pub where the Secret Rozzer has been stealing information? For your podcast. You might not be the voice, but you told the world about how Miss Carnegie sexually abused me.' He's gritting his teeth. 'Why? Why did you do it? Why?'

Thing is, I don't have an answer. All this shite for nothing.

But sod it, Thornton wanted to recruit Hunter and Cullen. Use their muscle and their brains. Chantal and Yvonne getting threats like I had and Malky.

Malky's dead.

Christ.

And if these two pricks aren't about, Thornton doesn't have a use for me. I've got one chance here. Kill them, buy myself some time to free Apinya.

I should do this. Right now.

Get rid of Cullen and Hunter.

Why am I getting cold feet?

Is it because it's Cullen? My Sundance? The lad I groomed from DC to DI?

Maybe.

I point the rifle at Hunter. 'Sorry, big man. This is for kicking the shite out of us in that phone box.'

29

CULLEN

Cullen could only stand and watch.

Bain pressed the gun to Hunter's chest. 'Down on your knees.'

Hunter laughed at Bain, his face all bloody. 'Fine.' He went down on one knee, then dropped the other. 'I should've kicked the shite out of you years ago, Brian. You're a spineless creep. Nobody likes you. Nobody respects you. And you were useless as a cop.'

Bain was snarling. 'Shut up.'

'Kill me, then.' Hunter looked over at Thornton. 'Show your boss how hardcore you are.'

Bain glanced over.

Cullen snatched the opportunity, lashing forward and smashing his dangling handcuffs into Bain's face.

Bain dropped the gun. 'Ah, you bastard!'

Two choices—go for the gun or Hunter.

Cullen pulled Hunter away and got him to his feet. 'We need to get out of here!' He ran towards the entrance, then glanced back the way.

Bain picked up the rifle and was aiming it right at them.

'Down!' Cullen grabbed Hunter and pushed him over.

The rifle barked out a round.

Hunter screamed.

Cullen tumbled over and hit his face off the rough floor.

Hunter was rubbing at his shoulder. It was a mess, all bloody with subcutaneous fat leaking out.

Bain stood over them, training the gun on Cullen. 'Kill you first, actually.'

Cullen shuffled back against an upright, then stared down the barrel of the gun at Bain.

Hunter had tried to fight fire with fire, goad him, made him angry. It had worked then, but it wouldn't again.

Bain would just shoot.

Cullen needed to take a different tack. 'Brian, I'm sorry.'

'Sorry?' Bain laughed. 'What for?'

'For all you've been through. You've endured so much personal tragedy.'

'What are you talking about?'

'Your divorce. Your son letting you down. Your father's illness. His death. Your ex-wife's death. But you showed adversity amongst that. Finding love again with Apinya. She's lovely. And your daughter too. There's hope for you, Brian. A future.'

Thornton walked over to them. 'Brian, this is getting tiresome...'

Bain's finger slipped off the guard. It was working.

Cullen needed to double down here, get to whatever heart and soul was left in there. 'You helped define me and my career. I'm sorry they drummed you out of the force. That wasn't on me. I tried to keep you on. You need help and I'll—'

'Shut up!' Bain pulled the trigger.

The gun didn't fire.

Cullen felt a surge of relief flickering right up his chest. He gasped and sucked in the damp air.

Bain held the gun in front of his face. Then he started to shake and cry. He chucked the gun on the floor.

Thornton wagged his finger in the air. 'No, no, no.' He got his phone out and held it.

Live video showed Apinya answering the door. A man stood back, a gun tucked into his waistband.

'Just need to say the word, Brian, and my guys here will kill her.' Thornton reached into the locker and got out another gun. 'You're going to kill them.'

Hunter was lying on his back, staring up at the roof. Moaning. Blood pooled around his shoulder, soaking into the sawdust.

Bain looked at Cullen, his eyes wet, cheeks slimy, and held out his hand.

'Good man.' Thornton held the other rifle out for Bain. 'Finish the job.'

Cullen darted forward and stuck the nut on Thornton.

The gun dropped onto the sawdust and rolled.

Cullen pushed away and dived for the gun. Grabbed it. Raised it. Pointed it at Thornton.

But Thornton had an arm across Bain's throat, a pistol trained at his head. His own skull was hidden. 'To kill me, you have to kill him. Got the bollocks for that?'

Cullen looked around the room.

Bonzo was on his feet, pulling out a handgun.

The two lumps who carried out Nina were back, both armed.

Surrounded by henchmen.

To get away, Cullen had to shoot Bain to shoot Thornton. His body was mostly obscured by Bain, but Cullen could get his arm or his thigh. Then again, he was no marksman.

He'd get one shot at this.

If he was lucky, he'd kill Thornton, and the henchmen would give up.

Maybe.

But he had three guns trained on him.

'Got your back, Scott.' Somehow Hunter was on his feet, swinging Bain's dropped rifle at one of Thornton's goons, clubbing him with the butt and sending him tumbling backwards.

One of them spotted it and caught Hunter on the follow-through, cracking his own rifle into Hunter's face.

Hunter fell down at Cullen's feet.

A car pulled up nearby. More goons, no doubt.

Yep. Another two henchmen stepped into the barn, pointing guns at them.

No, Cullen was kidding himself. He had no options left here. If he killed Thornton, they'd die in a rain of gunfire the second Thornton dropped.

Cullen raised the gun to the ceiling. 'Okay, let's talk about us working for you.'

30

SHEPHERD

Shepherd drove forward along the uneven path, bucking and rolling, then stopped the car. Maybe two hundred metres away.

The lights were on in the farm, lighting up the grey morning.

Shepherd got out and waved down the other two cars. They both heeded his warning.

Sharon and Vicky were out first, jaws set tight.

The second car was filled with an Armed Response Unit. Four black-clad ninjas hopped out and started taking guns from the boot.

Shepherd put his binoculars to his eyes and trained them on the farm. Pretty far from the farmhouse, and out in the Lammermuir wilds. Nobody around for miles and miles.

Perfect place to kill people.

Close to Edinburgh to have a big enough catchment of victims.

Still, they'd made a schoolboy error. Should've dumped Bain's car when they had the chance.

But they hadn't.

'Okay.' Shepherd waited for the ARU to join them.

Two men, two women, all with that steely look that only came from being prepared to shoot to kill at a moment's notice.

'Let's get the lay of the land here. Priority is for no bloodshed.' Shepherd looked at Vicky. 'DI Dodds, you're with me. Rest of you hang back here. I want a sniper ready by the time we get over there. And await my orders before firing.'

'Sir.'

'Sir.'

'Sure.'

Sharon just nodded.

'Okay, let's do this.' Shepherd set off through the rain, splashing in the mud.

Bain's car was parked next to a big lorry. Maroon like the Hearts home shirt, but the signage was Hibs green. One of those ones that travelled all around Edinburgh, transporting God knows what.

Nobody around. Hard to see where to go from here, except some footprints in the mud led down towards a barn.

A muddy Subaru sat next to the lorry. Empty, but the engine still running.

Shepherd nodded at Vicky then set off.

Voices got louder as they neared. 'You've got stones, Cullen, that's for sure.'

Shepherd looked at Vicky—she'd heard them too. Cullen was alive. He let out a deep breath. Relief? Maybe.

'Could use someone with bollocks like that. Just lower the gun.'

'Your guys will just kill me.'

All Shepherd had on him was his baton, but he'd done this before. Many times.

He snaked around the side, hugging the wall of crates, until he could see inside.

Cullen and Hunter were both armed, both aiming at

Thornton, who stood behind Bain, using Bain's hand to aim a pistol at Cullen.

Some goons stood around the perimeter. All armed too.

Thornton shook his head. 'Scott, just lower the gun.'

Shepherd could approach from behind, easily, but he'd be seen by the others, and he'd become a target. He leaned over to Vicky. 'Go and get two of the ARU.'

'Sure about that?'

'Go.'

And she did.

Shepherd stayed where he was, trying to assess the probabilities.

Four goons, all aiming guns at Cullen.

Hunter on the deck.

Bain at Thornton's mercy.

Shepherd spotted two tarps just outside the far door. Rolled up, like there were bodies inside.

And Becky...

Becky was cowering in the corner.

It was a static situation now, seven people involved. A stand-off that would stay that way until someone was daft enough to break off.

Bain kept aiming the gun high, like he was resisting Thornton.

'Brian, for Christ's sake.' Thornton grabbed the pistol off Bain and pointed it at his head. 'I've had enough of you.'

Shepherd's static situation just got very dynamic.

He looked back the way. No sign of Vicky or the ARU.

He had to move. Now.

Shepherd ran forward. 'Police!'

Thornton looked around at Shepherd, but kept his gun on Bain. 'Who the hell are you?'

Aye, his baton felt so powerful right now with three guns aimed at him. 'Lay down your weapons. You are under arrest.'

Thornton just laughed.

But a red dot swam across the interior, landing on Thornton's leg. Another picked out one of his goons.

Thornton noticed it. Too late.

A shot rang out, whizzing past Shepherd's ear, and suckering Thornton's upper thigh. He went down, screaming like a pig.

But he still held the pistol.

He aimed it and fired.

Bain flew away from him like he'd been thrown by a giant.

The sound was deafening.

Another shot and a goon fell. Then another. Both screamed, clutching their arms.

Thornton swung around and took aim at Shepherd again. He squeezed the trigger, his face screwed up with menace.

A crack of gunfire and Thornton went down.

Over the other side of the barn, Hunter lay on the floor, holding the rifle Bain had tried to kill Cullen with. 'He'd jammed it. I clear the misfired cartridge and… Well.'

Cullen stood over Bain. What was left of him. 'This isn't going to be an open casket.'

EPILOGUE

Cullen
A while later

Davenport turned on the TV hanging from the wall. Craig Hunter sat in one of the interview rooms downstairs, covered in bandages and tape and plasters. Head bowed. Seemed like he'd been in hospital for months.

Interviewed by that Professional Standards pillock.

Cullen couldn't remember his name. Napier, maybe? No, Muir. Simon Muir. DS Simon Muir. How was he still there? The Complaints had a limited tenure, so he couldn't be longer than three years, max.

And still, he was sitting opposite Hunter, interviewing him.

Davenport switched off the screen and let out a sigh. 'Craig's future as a police officer is touch and go.'

Cullen swallowed down a thick lump of tears. He looked

over at Shepherd, staring into space and useless, then back at Davenport. 'There's nothing I can do to save his career?'

'He was unlucky, Scott. That's it.'

'He saved my life. He saved Luke's.'

'And we'll take that into account. Everyone talks shop out of here, especially when three sheets to the wind, but Craig just had the misfortune to be daft about it in Brian Bain's pub.'

Bain.

Christ.

Cullen swallowed more tears down. He cleared his throat. 'Speaking of which…' He looked over at Shepherd. 'Luke, it's time.'

Shepherd snapped to focus. 'Oh, right. Aye.'

∽

'JESUS, Luke, I don't want to be attending my own funeral.'

Shepherd weaved his way around another bend on the single-track road. A VW camper van careened towards them and Shepherd used the passing place to zap around the van in a squeal of horns. 'Relax, Scott. We'll be fine.' He indicated and took the next turning.

The garden was lush and filled with mature trees, all natives, completely at odds with the barren countryside.

The car park was largely empty, just a few cars.

Shepherd pulled up and they got out. 'Bang on time.'

'Bursting, though.'

'You can go after the service, Scott.'

'Kind of expected us to stop on the way up.'

'Getting from Edinburgh to here in just over two hours means we didn't need to stop.'

'Like to see how you get away with that one.' Cullen entered the crematorium.

The first row was filled, but that was pretty much it.

On one side, two big lumps sat together, flanked by even bigger lumps in prison guard uniforms. One of them looked around. Kieron Bain. Presumably out for the day. He'd bulked up big time. Next to him was Alan Irvine. All Cullen got was a glare.

Cullen took the opposite side, struggling to avoid looking at him. Shepherd shuffled in next to him, blocking his view. Thank God.

Apinya Bain was at the front, talking into the microphone. Her soft voice echoed around the cavernous room, making it hard to pick out words or even syllables. 'And that was my husband. A kind, gentle man, but with a fiery passion for justice.' She brushed away her tears, then stepped down, stopping to touch the closed casket.

Cullen's only reason to be here was to make sure he was actually dead. All the investigations undertaken by Shepherd's people and he hadn't been allowed anywhere near the body. He could be in there, waiting to jump out and it's all a joke.

The minister stood up, a short woman with silvery hair. 'Now, one of Brian's longstanding colleagues would like to read a eulogy. Scott Cullen.'

What the hell?

The sign at the side showed the service order.

Eulogy: Scott Cullen

Shepherd elbowed Cullen. 'On you go, Scott. They're all waiting.'

Cullen didn't have a choice, so he set off over and tried to think of anything to say. Nothing. He stepped up to the microphone and cleared his throat. 'So, I've worked with Brian for a few years, first in Lothian and Borders Police, then in Police Scotland. Ten years ago, he took me under his wing as a Detective Constable and was always...'

He looked around the sparse crowd, at Bain's son. His wife, his daughter. At Alan Irvine, who Cullen hadn't seen for a very long time. Never thought he would again.

Cullen smiled. 'He was always Bain. That's the thing. He was always himself. Didn't care about other people, really, about what they thought. I like to think in his head that he thought he was always doing the right thing too, catching the bad guys, just in his own way.'

Irvine was shaking his head. His guard whispered something in his ear.

'I didn't always like Brian, it's fair to say. We rarely saw eye to eye, but I wouldn't be standing here if it wasn't for him. A few years ago, I was almost shot, but he...' Cullen swallowed hard. 'He jumped in front of a flying bullet for me. Took the shot. Was in hospital for a while after. And I tried to see him but he wouldn't let me in. Then, next I know, he was back in Edinburgh, working as a sergeant, the same grade as me. That was strange. But... Stranger was when I was made a DI and he was working *for* me.'

'You're a DI?' Irvine was scowling. His guard grabbed his arm and whispered again.

'I was there when he died and—' Cullen caught a flash of Bain's death, the shot to the head, and felt like he was going to throw up. 'Well, he died a hero.'

A lie and he knew it. Bain died a coward and a traitor.

'So, I'll miss him now he's gone. It's been a weird old road for the last year and a bit, and I don't know what my life will be like without him.'

Cullen stepped down from the microphone, but couldn't go back to his seat just yet. He knew he had to open the casket. Prove to himself that Bain was gone, that this wasn't some elaborate joke.

So he opened it.

And, Christ, they'd done a good job. There he was. Bain. His final resting place. Dressed in a full Rangers kit from the nine-in-a-row season. Even wore muddy football boots a few sizes too big.

Cullen stared at him for a few seconds, wondering if he'd wake up. Say, 'Morning, Sundance.'

But no, he was dead. Gone.

Cullen shut the lid and walked back to his seat, clocking Elvis on his way past.

The minister took her place at the podium. 'Please rise for the body of Brian William Bain's final act on this Earth. He will meet his maker soon enough.'

The speakers crackled into life. Car horns squealed, then Tom Jones bellowed out 'You don't have to be beautiful to turn me on.'

Most people would settle for a dirge, but Bain had *Kiss* by The Art of Noise.

Cullen couldn't help but smile.

Christ.

What a guy.

Apinya was cradling their daughter, Kelya, but she was laughing. Happy tears, Cullen hoped. Maybe the song was as much a message of love to her, as it was a big piss off to everyone else.

The coffin was almost at the back of the conveyor belt now.

The coffin hit the edge just as the instrumental break started, then descended into the heat.

Brian Bain.

A one off.

And now gone.

'Women and girls rule my world.'

Christ.

The coffin popped out of view, lost to the burning flames.

The music faded to its conclusion and the minister stood up at the front. 'Thank you for your attendance. Apinya would like to invite you all to the Ruthven Arms Hotel for a celebration of her husband's life. Thank you. And may God be with you.'

The Corries started up, the stirring bagpipes of *Flower of Scotland*. As dead as Cullen was inside, he could feel the passion swelling in that song.

He got up and left the place, letting the cold air outside cool him down.

So much of his time on the police had been dealing with Bain.

Bain had saved Cullen's life eight years ago. Stopping Cullen dying and taking the blow from the knife himself.

But he'd tried to shoot him, just a broken machine gun saving his life.

The dreams Cullen had endured since, where the gun didn't jam. The bullets hitting him, waking him up.

And now it was over.

No more misery from that man. No more anything from him.

'Scott.' Apinya was out first, leading Kelya by the hand. The girl was looking like she was ready to start school. 'Thank you for coming and thank you for your eulogy. It was... Well, I'm sure he would've... found it interesting.'

'I'm sorry for your loss.' A cliché but it was all he had for her.

'A lot of people won't be, but he meant the world to me. I knew what he was, but I loved him anyway.'

'I understand. He died a hero.' Kind of.

'Thank you.' She reached over to stroke his cheek. 'Listen, I know he was a dick. I know the shite he was pulling with you. I can only apologise for it. I tried stopping him, but... I was fixing him, Scott. I just thought I'd have more time.'

Cullen stared into her eyes and saw the love she had for Bain, mixed with the disgust for his actions. And his antics.

He'd been playing games for a while, all while Cullen had been defending him.

The rest of the mourners started filing out.

Cullen gave her a nod. 'I'll see you around.'

'I hope not.' She smiled at Shepherd as he passed. 'Thanks for coming. Are you a colleague of Brian's?'

'Could say that. Sorry for your loss.' Shepherd smiled and set off with Cullen.

They walked back to the car in silence. Cullen's head was empty now.

'Sorry we missed it, Scott. Swear it was to start at half past.'

'It's fine. We tried. And we would've been really late if you hadn't broken all the speed limits on the way here.' Cullen got in the passenger seat and watched the crowd around Apinya.

Kieron and Irvine were closely guarded, then led towards the prison van. A long drive back to Perth for them.

'What next, Scott?'

Cullen shut his eyes and breathed in the new car smell. 'I don't know. Home. A beer and a bath.'

'I meant after this.'

'Been a hell of a hard time recently, that's for sure. Just go back to the MIT. I'll miss having you on my team, Luke.'

'I've got other dodgy cops to catch.'

'So many. Too many.'

Shepherd snorted. 'And I thought you were one, Scott. Believed it. It was hard to start with, because you'd come from under my wing. But... I was wrong to listen to Malky McKeown and to Brian Bain. You're a good cop. One of the best.'

'Thanks.' Cullen's ears burnt and he had to look away. 'But those two weren't the reason you were there. Who was it?'

'Davenport.'

Cullen nodded. It made sense. He'd never trusted him. Drummed him out of his team ten years ago into Bain's waiting arms. Still… 'It'll be tough working for someone who thinks I'm corrupt.'

'Maybe you should come work for me, Scott. Tour Scotland and take down bent cops.'

Cullen looked around at him. 'Are you serious?'

'It'll be fun. Very different to what you've done in your career so far.'

WILL CULLEN RETURN?

Maybe. But not for a wee while.

I've done six of these in the last eighteen months, so I'll give the poor sod a wee break and then torture him some more.

I'm giving myself 2022 to focus on new stuff, standalones and some new series. I hope you enjoy them.

If you sign up to my mailing list, you'll get access to **free, exclusive** content and be up-to-speed with all of my releases:

https://geni.us/EJmailer

And, in case you missed it, I published a Vicky Dodds prequel novella in April 2021. Get it in paperback or for FREE on Kindle here:

Next book

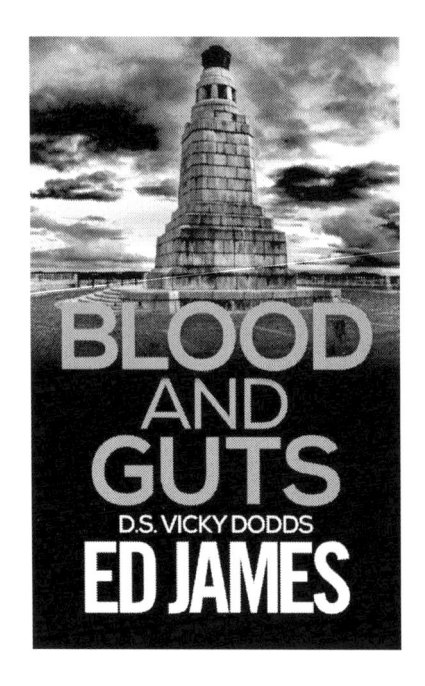

https://geni.us/EJDoback

Printed in Great Britain
by Amazon